SWEET
PERSECUTION

SWEET PERSECUTION

A 30-Day Devotional
With Reflections From
the Persecuted Church

by Ron Brackin
foreword by Johan Companjen

BETHANY HOUSE PUBLISHERS
MINNEAPOLIS, MINNESOTA 55438

Published by Bethany House Publishers
11400 Hampshire Avenue South
Minneapolis, Minnesota 55438
www.bethanyhouse.com

Library of Congress Cataloging-in-Publication Data

Brackin, Ron.
    Sweet persecution / by Ron Brackin.
       p. cm.
    ISBN 0–7642–2285–6 (pbk.)
    1. Persecution—Prayer-books and devotions—English. 2. Devotional calendars. I. Title.
BR1602.B73   1999   99–6559
242'.2—dc21   CIP

Dedication

When he opened the fifth seal, I saw under the altar the souls of those who had been slain because of the word of God and the testimony they had maintained. (Revelation 6:9)

To these faithful brothers and sisters, this book is gratefully and affectionately dedicated.

RON BRACKIN, a former broadcast journalist, then congressional press secretary in Washington, D.C., has served the past eight years as a free-lance writer and fund-raiser for many major Christian ministries, including Open Doors International with Brother Andrew. He is the author of two books and numerous newspaper and magazine feature articles. He and his wife, Annie, live in Texas with their four children.

Fear not, for I am with thee.

Foreword

Someone once said that if you took suffering out of the New Testament, it would be a very thin book. In *Sweet Persecution*, our friend Ron Brackin takes us into the New Testament to see for ourselves what the Word says about persecution. Add to this the testimonies and stories from our brothers and sisters who make up the suffering church, and we have a powerful message.

But is persecution ever sweet? Recently in Sudan, my wife and I met with a sister in Christ whose husband was in prison for his faith. She had been beaten with twenty lashes of a camel whip when she dared to challenge the system that condemned her husband. We will never forget the look on her face when we dared to ask her whether she would do it all again.

Open Doors International has been ministering to the persecuted, suffering church for almost forty-five years, but it is only in recent times that the church in the Western world has begun to wake up to the fact that the body of Christ is under siege. For us, persecution is not the latest buzz word but an ongoing challenge to make the plight of the church known. Hence this devotional.

Read it and be challenged by it. We have a duty to remember those in prison as though we are imprisoned too. I cannot recall the number of times I have heard these words when visiting Christians on the front lines: "We thought we had been forgotten. . . ." Sometimes just being there and giving them a shoulder to cry on is all they need.

—Johan Companjen,
    President, Open Doors
    International

Contents

Introduction

The New Testament is the story of God's single greatest act of love. But it is also the account of His *second* greatest act of love.

The first was sending His only Son to pay the unimaginable price for our sins. The second was allowing His redeemed children—you and me—to suffer and die for the name of His Son.

Western Christianity today has no theology of persecution. Ours is a theology of prosperity—a faith without risk and a salvation that does little more than snatch us away from the rim of hell, pat us on the back, and send us on our way with our heavenly ticket punched.

The Bible, however, paints a radically different picture.

While believers in the West joyfully quote the litany of mighty heroes of the faith in Hebrews 11:1–35, the church throughout the rest of the world daily experiences the reality of verses 35–38:

> Others were tortured and refused to be released, so that they might gain a better resurrection. Some faced jeers and flogging, while still others were chained and put in prison. They were stoned; they were sawed in two; they were put to death by the sword. They went about in sheepskins and goatskins, destitute, persecuted and mistreated—the world was not worthy of them. They wandered in deserts and mountains, and in caves and holes in the ground.

Persecution is inevitable. It is just as much of what Watchman Nee calls "the normal Christian life" as prayer, worship, and fellowship.

We love to claim the blessings of Matthew 5:3–9 but preach little on verses 10–12:

> Blessed are those who are persecuted because of righteousness, for theirs is the kingdom of heaven. Blessed are you when people insult you, persecute you and falsely say all kinds of evil against you because of me. Rejoice and be glad, because great is your reward in heaven, for in the same way they persecuted the prophets who were before you.

Can I hear an *amen*, somebody?

We cannot embrace the blessings of being Christ's and spurn the persecution. The rule is: first the persecution, then the blessing.

> "I tell you the truth," Jesus replied, "no one who has left home or brothers or sisters or mother or father or children or fields for me and the gospel will fail to receive a hundred times as much in this present age (homes, brothers, sisters, mothers, children and fields—*and with them, persecutions*) and in the age to come, eternal life" (Mark 10:29–30).

Do we expect to get back a hundred times more than what we give up for Jesus? Of course we do. And we will. With persecutions.

Do we expect to enter the kingdom of God? Of course we do.

> They preached the good news in that city and won a large number of disciples. Then they returned to Lystra, Iconium and Antioch, strengthening the disciples and encouraging them to remain true to the faith. "We must go through many hardships to enter the kingdom of God," they said. (Acts 14:21–22)

Do we want Jesus to be manifest in our lives? Certainly.

> We are hard pressed on every side, but not crushed; perplexed, but not in despair; persecuted, but not abandoned; struck down, but not destroyed. We always carry around in our body the death of Jesus, so that the life of Jesus may also be revealed in our body. For we who are alive are always being given over to death for Jesus' sake, so that his life may be revealed in our mortal body. (2 Corinthians 4:8–11)

Do we want to live godly lives in Christ Jesus? Absolutely.

Again Paul explains to his friends that they . . .

... know all about my teaching, my way of life, my purpose, faith, patience, love, endurance, persecutions, sufferings—what kinds of things happened to me in Antioch, Iconium and Lystra, the persecutions I endured. Yet the Lord rescued me from all of them. In fact, *everyone who wants to live a godly life in Christ Jesus will be persecuted*. (2 Timothy 3:10–12)

All right, so blessings follow persecution. But where does it say that persecution is inevitable?

"*When* you are persecuted . . ." (Matthew 10:23).

"*When* trouble or persecution comes because of the word . . ." (Matthew 13:21).

"Then you *will* be handed over to be persecuted and put to death, and you *will* be hated by all nations because of me" (Matthew 24:9).

" 'We *must* go through many hardships to enter the kingdom of God,' they said" (Acts 14:22).

"In fact, everyone who wants to live a godly life in Christ Jesus *will* be persecuted . . ." (2 Timothy 3:12).

And Jesus says in Revelation 2:10,

"Do not be afraid of what you are about to suffer. I tell you, the devil will put some of you in prison to test you, and you will suffer persecution for ten days. Be faithful, even to the point of death, and I will give you the crown of life."

Finally, no one denies that Jesus himself was persecuted—beyond anything we can ever imagine or understand. And He says clearly in John 15:20, "Remember the words I spoke to you: 'No servant is greater than his master.' If they persecuted me, they will persecute you also."

Persecution is inevitable in the life of every Christian, whether it takes the form of beatings, imprisonment, and martyrdom or, as is more common in the West, in the form of temptations.

No temptation has seized you except what is common to man. And God is faithful; he will not let you be tempted beyond what you can bear. But *when you are tempted*, he will also provide a way out so that you can stand up under it. (1 Corinthians 10:13)

Seized you . . . tempted beyond what you can bear . . . a way out . . . stand up under it. Doesn't this sound like persecution?

But recognizing that persecution is normal and unavoidable is just the first step.

In this thirty-day devotional, we will look at persecution from God's perspective. And we will read true stories of the modern-day faith and courage of our brothers and sisters around the world—many of whom are paying the highest price for following Jesus.

How to Use This Devotional

Sweet Persecution is useful for personal study, prayer, and meditation, as well as for Sunday school, group Bible studies, or home groups. It is also an ideal thirty-day preparation for the annual International Day of Prayer for the Persecuted Church, which occurs mid-November.

Each day begins with a selected Bible text, followed by a true story of faith in the face of persecution that will strengthen and encourage you, provide a touchpoint for your prayers, and remind you of the urgent needs of the church in countries that are hostile to the Gospel.

Following each story are *A Few Observations*. These are not meant to be a comprehensive teaching, but some thoughts to help stimulate meditation or discussion.

The *Food for Thought* section is just that. It is designed to give you a little more to chew on; to help you or your group apply to your own life the principles highlighted by the devotion.

And *For Further Study* offers Scriptures that expand on and reinforce what is presented each day.

Occasionally, *Sweet Persecution* also recommends other books or group activities to help strengthen your understanding of and relationship to the persecuted church.

"Is persecution ever sweet?" Johann asks in the Foreword to this book. Definitely not in the sense of the pain and loss suffered. But it is indeed sweet in a much deeper sense—the sense experienced by the apostles who, after being flogged, "left the Sanhedrin *rejoicing* because they had been counted worthy of suffering disgrace for the Name" (Acts 5:41).

My deepest desire and earnest prayer is that, after you read this little devotional, fear of any form of persecution will have no place in you. That condemnation will find no foothold in your soul when you find yourself suffering for no apparent reason. That you will be bolder for Christ's sake than ever before, caring nothing for whatever you might suffer in consequence.

I pray, as Peter prayed, that you will "not be surprised at the painful trial you are suffering, as though something strange were happening to you. But *rejoice* that you participate in the sufferings of Christ, so that you may be *overjoyed* when his glory is revealed. If you are insulted because of the name of Christ, you are *blessed*, for the Spirit of glory and of God rests on you. If you suffer, it should not be as a murderer or thief or any other kind of criminal, or even as a meddler. However, if you suffer as a Christian, do not be ashamed, but *praise God* that you bear that name" (1 Peter 4:12–16).

Finally, I hope that you will add the men, women, and children of the persecuted church worldwide to your permanent prayer list. That they would be in your heart and on your lips not only one day of the year but every day.

And that, as a result of your prayers and mine, our suffering brothers and sisters would feel in the midst of their persecution, "how wide and long and high and deep is the love of Christ, and to know this love that surpasses knowledge" that they "may be filled to the measure of all the fullness of God" (Ephesians 3:18–19).

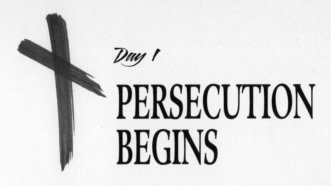

PERSECUTION BEGINS

After Jesus was born in Bethlehem in Judea, during the time of King Herod, Magi from the east came to Jerusalem and asked, "Where is the one who has been born king of the Jews? We saw his star in the east and have come to worship him." When King Herod heard this he was disturbed, and all Jerusalem with him.

(MATTHEW 2:1–3)

Dr. Paul Negrut pastored the largest Baptist church in Europe, located in Oradea, Romania. He served the church faithfully under the cruel Ceausescu regime and often suffered personal mistreatment.

One night, after a very successful evangelistic crusade, he returned home to find his wife weeping and his nine-year-old daughter trembling.

Through her tears, his wife explained that when their daughter was coming home from school, the Securitate (secret police) tried to rape her to destroy her and the family.

"That night I was in a great struggle," Paul said. "For the first time I was thinking to emigrate from Romania. I asked the Lord, 'Should I leave the blessing of suffering or should I endure to see my girl like that?'

"I talked to my wife, and we chose to stay.

"Two days later, they tried again to rape my daughter. And two days later they tried to rape my wife. But every time God was protecting them in a miraculous way."[1]

A Few Observations

The persecution of the church began before it was even established. It started when Satan stirred up the fear, greed, and rage in the heart of a man named Herod and wielded him like a sword to pierce the heart of Jesus. If he could destroy this Messiah as soon as He arrived, Satan thought, there would be no church, no cross, and no redemption. And Satan would win his war against God.

But Jesus was not alone on this earth. His Father was with Him, watching over and protecting Him. And God sent an angel to warn Joseph and Mary to escape. Satan tried many other times during Jesus' life to stop Him from reaching the cross.

He used temptations, riotous Jews, proud religious leaders, and finally, when all seemed lost, Satan used the spirit of rejection that caused Jesus to cry out, " 'Eloi, Eloi, lama sabachthani?'—which means, 'My God, my God, why have you forsaken me?' " (Matthew 27:46).

There was, however, no persecution that could separate Jesus from the love of His Father. He did indeed accomplish His mission. And from that time to this, Satan has turned his hatred against the church—Christ's physical body on earth.

Food for Thought

Every Christian has a unique mission on earth. How has Satan used persecution to discourage you from accomplishing your mission? Persistent temptations? Life-threatening accidents? Choices that led you in the opposite direction from the way God would have you go? Persecution by family members, your community, classmates, co-workers, government officials?

For Further Study

Jesus was not the only one the devil tried to kill in his youth. Satan used this strategy over and over throughout the Old Testament.

- Read Genesis 37 to see how Satan used Joseph's jealous brothers to try to destroy the child and prevent the birth of the nation of Israel in Egypt.
- Read Exodus 1 and 2 and watch Satan use Egypt's pharaoh to try to destroy the fledgling nation of Israel—and Israel's newborn deliverer, Moses.
- And in 1 Samuel 17 and 18, Satan used a bear, a lion, a giant Philistine warrior, and even a king of Israel to try to kill a boy named David and destroy the God-ordained lineage of Jesus.
- In the book of Esther, Satan uses wicked Haman to try to kill the beautiful young Esther and destroy the remnant of Israel.

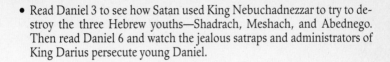

- Read Daniel 3 to see how Satan used King Nebuchadnezzar to try to destroy the three Hebrew youths—Shadrach, Meshach, and Abednego. Then read Daniel 6 and watch the jealous satraps and administrators of King Darius persecute young Daniel.

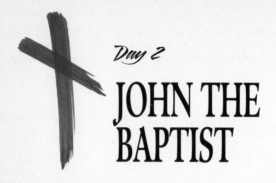

Day 2

JOHN THE BAPTIST

For Herod himself had given orders to have John arrested, and he had him bound and put in prison. He did this because of Herodias, his brother Philip's wife, whom he had married. For John had been saying to Herod, "It is not lawful for you to have your brother's wife." So Herodias nursed a grudge against John and wanted to kill him. But she was not able to, because Herod feared John and protected him, knowing him to be a righteous and holy man. When Herod heard John, he was greatly puzzled; yet he liked to listen to him.

Finally the opportune time came. On his birthday Herod gave a banquet for his high officials and military commanders and the leading men of Galilee. When the daughter of Herodias came in and danced, she pleased Herod and his dinner guests.

The king said to the girl, "Ask me for anything you want, and I'll give it to you." And he promised her with an oath, "Whatever you ask I will give you, up to half my kingdom." She went out and said to her mother, "What shall I ask for?" "The head of John the Baptist," she answered. At once the girl hurried in to the king with the request: "I want you to give me right now the head of John the Baptist on a platter."

The king was greatly distressed, but because of his oaths and his dinner guests, he did not want to refuse her. So he immediately sent an executioner with orders to bring John's head. The man went, beheaded John in the prison, and brought back his head on a platter. He presented it to the girl, and she gave it to her mother. On hearing of this, John's disciples came and took his body and laid it in a tomb.

(MARK 6:17–29)

Korean Elder Kwan-Joon Park was called an "Elijah of Korea" or sometimes a "Daniel of modern times."

He died as a martyr for his faith in Christ and for his opposition to the Japanese colonial rule during World War II, when Korea was occupied by the Japanese Imperialists. The latter enforced Shinto worship on the Korean people.

On March 24, 1939, Elder Park went to Japan to protest against the inhuman colonial policies of Japan.

He walked into the 74th Imperial Diet. And when the opening pronouncement of the lower house was made, he rose from his seat in the visitor's balcony and shouted, "This is a great mission of God, Jehovah's great message!"

Then he threw leaflets to the floor below, exposing the cruel abuse of Korean Christians by Japan and warning them of God's imminent judgment. The leaflets also explained the resistance against Japan's imposition of Shinto shrine worship upon Korean Christians.

Elder Park was arrested and sentenced to six years in Japanese prison. At the age of seventy, while serving his sentence, Elder Park was martyred.

A line from his last poem written in prison reads,

Since Jesus died for me, I will die for Jesus![2]

A Few Observations

Jesus was the first new creation (2 Corinthians 5:17) to be persecuted, but He was far from the last. Everyone associated with Him—everyone who accepts and follows His teaching—should expect the same treatment.

In fact, so great is the devil's hatred of God's people that he struck out against all that were His—before and after Jesus. And Satan used many different weapons.

Although another Herod was in power in Israel, it was not he who wielded the sword against John the Baptist. This time, the devil used a woman—Herod's wife, Herodias.

In fact, John's death was an amazing replay of an act of persecution that took place centuries before. Inside Herodias was the same murderous spirit that was in Jezebel, just as the spirit of Elijah was in John (Matthew 17:11–13; 1 Kings 19:1–2). Where Jezebel failed, however, Herodias succeeded.

A church that is not being persecuted is often one that tolerates sin. The church that knows it needs the love of Christ will sound the alarm and point sinners away from the flames toward safety.

Food for Thought

1. When the apostle Paul was struck down on the way to Damascus, Jesus said, "I am Jesus of Nazareth whom you are persecuting" (Acts 22:8). He did not say, "whom you once persecuted." How is Jesus still being persecuted even though He is bodily in heaven with our Father?

2. Herodias was driven by pride that would not admit wrongdoing and perhaps by the lust for power and wealth and the fear of losing it. This turned into hatred for the one who threatened it all with the truth. What other spirits and motives drive people and governments to persecute Christians? Have you ever been persecuted for speaking the truth?

For Further Study

- Read in Genesis 4 how *jealousy* caused Cain to murder his brother.
- 1 King 21 illustrates how *greed* drove Ahab to murder Naboth.
- Read in 2 Samuel 11 how David murdered Uriah out of *lust* for his wife.
- In Acts 22:3–5, Paul tells how he murdered Christians out of *religious zeal*.

Day 3

REJECTED BY NEIGHBORS

"I tell you the truth," he continued, "no prophet is accepted in his hometown. . . ." All the people in the synagogue were furious when they heard this. They got up, drove him out of the town, and took him to the brow of the hill on which the town was built, in order to throw him down the cliff. But he walked right through the crowd and went on his way.

(LUKE 4:24, 28–30)

Dr. John Pitt shares the poignant story of a young Christian named Timothy whom he met in Egypt.

Through the Christian radio broadcasts of Transworld Radio, Timothy asked Jesus into his heart and began to follow Him with great joy. But when he shared his new faith with his Muslim family, he was told to leave home and never to come back.

After several years of living with other Christians, he decided to try to reestablish contact with his family. On his mother's birthday, he bought some flowers and walked to his family's home. When he knocked on the door, his mother opened it.

"Happy birthday, Mother," Timothy said. "I brought you these flowers because I love you!"

"I don't know who you are!" she said sternly and slammed the door.

"I don't have a family anymore," Timothy told John later, his voice choked with emotion and tears streaming down his face. Then he looked at John and asked, "Will you be my family?"[3]

A Few Observations

Unlike those who are martyred or imprisoned for their faith, many Christians suffer persecution at the hands of family and neighbors—sometimes even fellow believers—in the form of rejection.

So it was with Jesus.

After He spoke in the synagogue where He grew up in Nazareth, "All spoke well of him and were amazed at the gracious words that came from his lips" (Luke 4:22). Then we can almost see them do a double take.

Wait a minute!

> "Where did this man get this wisdom and these miraculous powers?" they asked. "Isn't this the carpenter's son? Isn't his mother's name Mary, and aren't his brothers James, Joseph, Simon and Judas? Aren't all his sisters with us? Where then did this man get all these things?" And they took offense at him. (Matthew 13:54–57)

Today, we are often accused and taunted by the same religious spirit. "Who do you think you are," it shouts out of the mouths of unbelievers, "claiming to talk to God and hear from God? You're just an old sinner like us."

Or even, "We've sat next to you in a pew for years. Suddenly, you're a personal friend of God's?"

People with such a spirit will always oppose and persecute true believers.

Food for Thought

Many Western believers find that those least receptive to the Gospel are those closest to them, members of their own family. Have you experienced this? Have you suffered persecution from family members, neighbors, or co-workers on account of your faith?

For Further Study

- Those closest to us are sometimes the ones most likely to turn against us, as Delilah betrayed Samson (Judges 16), as David spoke of in Psalm 41:9 and 55:12–14, as the prophet warns in Micah 7:6, as Judas betrayed Christ (Matthew 26:23), and as Demas and Alexander deserted and betrayed Paul (2 Timothy 4:10, 14).
- The simplicity of the Gospel is another reason Christians are persecuted. "For the preaching of the cross is to them that perish foolishness; but unto us which are saved it is the power of God" (1 Corinthians 1:18 KJV).

DISCIPLES HATED

If the world hates you, keep in mind that it hated me first. If you belonged to the world, it would love you as its own. As it is, you do not belong to the world, but I have chosen you out of the world. That is why the world hates you. . . . They will put you out of the synagogue; in fact, a time is coming when anyone who kills you will think he is offering a service to God. They will do such things because they have not known the Father or me. I have told you this, so that when the time comes you will remember that I warned you.

(JOHN 15:18–19; 16:2–4)

As Dr. Paul Negrut entered the home of his old friend Trian Dors, he saw that Trian was bleeding from open wounds.

"What happened?" Paul asked.

"The secret police just left my home," Trian said. "They confiscated my manuscripts. Then they beat me."

When Paul began to complain about the heavy tactics of the secret police, Trian stopped him. "Brother Paul, it is so sweet to suffer for Jesus. God didn't bring us together tonight to complain but to praise Him. Let's kneel down and pray."

Trian knelt and began praying for the Securitate, asking God to bless and save them. He told God how much he loved them.

"God," Trian prayed, "if they will come back in the next few days, I pray that you will prepare me to minister to them."

By this time, Paul was ashamed. He thought he had been living the most difficult life in Romania for the Lord.

Trian then shared with Paul how the secret police had been coming to his home regularly for several years. They beat him twice every week. They confiscated all his papers.

After every beating, he would talk to the officer in charge. Looking into the officer's eyes, he would say, "Mister, I love you, and I want you to know that if our next meeting is before the judgment throne of God, you will not go to hell because I hate you but because you rejected love."

Years later, that officer came alone to his home one night. Trian prepared himself for another beating, but the officer spoke kindly and said, "Mr. Dors, the next time we meet will be before the judgment throne of God. I came tonight to apologize for what I did to you and to tell you that your love moved my heart. I have asked Christ to save me. But two days ago, the doctor discovered that I have a very severe case of cancer and have only a few weeks to live before I go to be with God. I came tonight to tell you that we will be together on the other side."[4]

A Few Observations

Jesus says the world hates His disciples. Again and again, He uses the word "hate." The Greek verb *miseo* means hating so intensely that one can find relief only by aggressively persecuting the object of the hatred.

In fact, Jesus explains in John 16:2 that this hatred is so strong that killing a Christian seems like doing God service. The word *latrela*, translated as "service," refers to divine service, that is, worship. In the mind of the world, then, killing a believer is an act of worship.

Jesus also makes it clear that those who have favor with the world—that is, those who agree with the world's belief system, morals, and values—are not the Lord's. From their perspective, they're getting along just fine and cannot understand what all the fuss is about. *Why can't Christians just go with the flow? Why do they have to be so stiff-necked, intolerant, and uncompromising?* the world wonders. *They're just trying to make everyone else look bad.*

Not really. We all look fine in our own mirrors. But when we stand next to Jesus, we can only fall on our faces and cry out, "Lord, have mercy on me, a sinner!" The true Christian does not judge; he merely reflects the righteousness of Christ.

Food for Thought

1. Suffering and persecution are rarely part of our Gospel presentation in the West. They are not part of the "four spiritual laws." Do you include them when you witness? Do you think they will scare people off and keep them

from receiving Christ? Do you think people should be told anyway?

2. When you were led to Christ, was *miseo* and persecution part of the Gospel you heard? Is this the first time you are hearing this? If you had known that suffering and persecution were part of the deal, would you still have embraced Christ? Do you have second thoughts now?

For Further Study

That the world hates Jesus' disciples is natural and inevitable. But what must our response be?

> "You have heard that it was said, 'Love your neighbor and hate your enemy.' But I tell you: Love your enemies and pray for those who persecute you" (Matthew 5:43–44).
>
> "Blessed are you when men hate you, when they exclude you and insult you and reject your name as evil, because of the Son of Man. Rejoice in that day and leap for joy, because great is your reward in heaven" (Luke 6:22–23).

Describing his struggle with sin, the apostle Paul says, "I do not understand what I do. For what I want to do I do not do, but what I hate I do" (Romans 7:15).

In other words, we are to *miseo* sin at the same time that we love and bless those who *miseo* us.

Day 5

PETER
AND JOHN

The priests and the captain of the temple guard and the Sadducees came up to Peter and John while they were speaking to the people. They were greatly disturbed because the apostles were teaching the people and proclaiming in Jesus the resurrection of the dead. They seized Peter and John, and because it was evening, they put them in jail until the next day. . . .

They ordered them to withdraw from the Sanhedrin and then conferred together. "What are we going to do with these men?" they asked. "Everybody living in Jerusalem knows they have done an outstanding miracle, and we cannot deny it. But to stop this thing from spreading any further among the people, we must warn these men to speak no longer to anyone in this name."

Then they called them in again and commanded them not to speak or teach at all in the name of Jesus. But Peter and John replied, "Judge for yourselves whether it is right in God's sight to obey you rather than God. For we cannot help speaking about what we have seen and heard."

(ACTS 4:1–3, 15–20)

Manuel was an effective evangelist among the Quechua Indians in the Andes.

One day, Shining Path guerrillas stopped him on the trail and told him to stop going to the mountains, stop handing out Bibles, cassettes, and other Christian materials, and stop preaching about Jesus. Or else.

Some weeks later, Manuel's body was found on the trail. His feet, hands, and tongue had been cut off. With a knife, they had carved on his torso the message: "We told you to stop . . ." And on the severed limbs, the message was completed: ". . . visiting the villages, distributing Bibles, preaching about Jesus!"[5]

A Few Observations

Few things will bring down persecution on a Christian more surely than talking to others about Jesus.

In many countries that oppose the Gospel, Christians are allowed to meet, pray, worship, read their Bibles (if they have any), and discuss Jesus *among themselves*. But they are not permitted to tell others about Him. In some countries, evangelizing unbelievers is punishable by imprisonment, even death. Even in the United States, it is unlawful to talk about Jesus in state-subsidized schools.

In recent years, some Christians have even been arrested, fined, and jailed for talking about Him on public streets. And discussing Him with co-workers is increasingly being considered a form of illegal harassment.

Food for Thought

Have you ever been persecuted for talking about Jesus? Do you know of anyone else who has? What if the government outlawed evangelism in your country? Would you obey, or become an outlaw and suffer the consequences?

For Further Study

The book of Acts is filled with examples of persecution.

- Read Acts 5:17–42 to see what happened when Peter and the other apostles disobeyed the warning of the religious leaders.
- Acts 6:8–7:60 is a powerful story of the church's first martyr, a young man named Stephen, whose death launched a widespread persecution—and phenomenal growth—of the fledgling church.
- Read Acts 12:1–19, which tells of another time that Peter was arrested and how God strengthened the persecuted church through Peter's miraculous release.
- Acts 16:16–40 is the incredible story of how God used the imprisonment of Paul and Silas to confound the religious leaders and bring salvation to all the inmates, as well as to the jailer and his entire family.
- And you can read about many other persecutions of Paul: at Antioch (Acts 13:50), Iconium (Acts 14:5), Lystra (Acts 14:19–20), Thessalonica (Acts 17:5), Berea (Acts 17:13), Corinth (Acts 18:6), Greece (Acts 20:3), and Jerusalem (Acts 21:27).

Suggested Activity

Many believers throughout the world are in prison for their faith. Conditions are harsh and sometimes deadly. Prisoners are fortunate to get one meal a day. To help you identify with your suffering brothers and sisters in prison, try to live without a favorite item (the newspaper, sodas, desserts, etc.) for a week or more.

Day 6

SWEET PERSECUTION

[We] rejoice in our sufferings, because we know that suffering produces perseverance; perseverance, character; and character, hope. And hope does not disappoint us, because God has poured out his love into our hearts by the Holy Spirit, whom he has given us.

(ROMANS 5:3–5)

Freddie Sun spent years in prison in China because of his Christian faith.

Prison was literally a trial of fire for him. He worked in a factory making tee joints from pig iron. Every day he loaded and unloaded the furnace, which fired up to 2,700°F (1482°C). In the midst of this hell on earth, God spoke to him.

"I have put you in this high-temperature furnace. Don't worry. You won't melt, but your impurities will be removed, so you can become a useful tee joint!"[6]

A Few Observations

In God's kingdom, persecution is to a believer like a blast furnace is to iron.

At about 3,000°F, a blast furnace melts down scrap iron, iron ore, and limestone in the checker chamber and turns it to steel. Alloy materials are added when the molten steel is tapped from the furnace. The slag floats to the surface of the steel and is drawn off, and the steel is teemed (poured) into ingot molds.

To be used, the steel ingots are rolled into sheets. They're removed from their molds and soaked in a pit at about 2,250°F until they are white hot and soft. Then they are squeezed long and flat between several sets of heavy rollers.

The steel is hardened for different purposes through tempering. Tempering actually changes the internal structure of the metal. After the steel is heated to a very high temperature, it is quenched, or rapidly cooled by plunging it into water, oil, or other liquid. The steel is then heated again to a temperature lower than before it was quenched and allowed to cool slowly. The temperatures determine the toughness.

So, too, God controls the amount and degree of persecution suffered by each of His children according to His plans and purposes. The strongest believers are those who have been greatly tempered.

Food for Thought

In 1 Corinthians 10:13, Paul assures us that "No temptation has seized you except what is common to man. And God is faithful; he will not let you be tempted beyond what you can bear. But when you are tempted, he will also provide a way out so that you can stand up under it." And Jesus himself says to Paul and to all of us, "My grace is sufficient for you, for my power is made perfect in weakness" (2 Corinthians 12:9).

Discuss ways that God has provided for you to escape temptation or bear up under persecution, and how His strength has sustained you in your weakness.

For Further Study

- Another purpose for persecution is what God describes as purging or pruning. In John 15:2, Jesus says, "He cuts off every branch in me that bears no fruit, while every branch that does bear fruit he prunes so that it will be even more fruitful."
- "He knows the way that I take; when he has tested me, I will come forth as gold" (Job 23:10).
- King David rejoices in that "before I was afflicted I went astray, but now I obey your word" (Psalm 119:67).
- And Hebrews 12:11 acknowledges that "no discipline seems pleasant at the time, but painful. Later on, however, it produces a harvest of righteousness and peace for those who have been trained by it."

Suggested Activity

Millions of Christians, particularly in China, do not own a personal copy of God's Word. Those who are blessed enough to own a Bible read aloud while others listen, copy the Scriptures by hand, and then memorize them. Many have copied the entire Bible.

To help you identify with your persecuted brethren, copy a chapter out of your Bible by hand. If you are reading this devotional as a member of a small group, "borrow" a Bible from a friend and copy out a chapter. Then pass the Bible from person to person until everyone has had the opportunity to copy the chapter. Depending on the number of people in your group and the "intensity of the persecution," this may be done during a meeting or take place between meetings with believers going to one another's homes to hand off the Bible, returning it finally to your friend. Once you finish copying your chapter, you will need to find a safe hiding place for it to avoid being arrested and having it confiscated.

Day 7

BELIEVER'S PROFILE

For it seems to me that God has put us apostles on display at the end of the procession, like men condemned to die in the arena. We have been made a spectacle to the whole universe, to angels as well as to men. We are fools for Christ, but you are so wise in Christ! We are weak, but you are strong! You are honored, we are dishonored! To this very hour we go hungry and thirsty, we are in rags, we are brutally treated, we are homeless. We work hard with our own hands. When we are cursed, we bless; when we are persecuted, we endure it; when we are slandered, we answer kindly. Up to this moment we have become the scum of the earth, the refuse of the world. . . . Therefore I urge you to imitate me.

(1 CORINTHIANS 4:9–13, 16)

Wilson Chen was sentenced to five years in a harsh, primitive Vietnamese reeducation camp. By day, he and the other prisoners were forced to spend long hours of backbreaking work clearing the jungle, cutting trees, and farming the fields. Every night, they were subjected to mental torture and political indoctrination. Always in their minds were thoughts of escape.

Camp food was barely enough to keep them alive. "The constant brutality attacked our minds and spirits," Wilson recalled. "The malnutrition attacked our bodies."

Gnawing hunger drove the prisoners to eat anything. Wilson searched the ground with other prisoners for rats, toads, worms, snakes, and insects to supplement their diet, keep them alive, and simply ease the pain of endless hunger.

He remembers companions who went insane from hunger. Others committed suicide. Many died of diseases caused by the malnutrition.

Wilson had looked forward to a successful secular career and to marrying his lovely girlfriend. In his final year in camp, though, he received the crushing news that she had given up hope, married another, and escaped from Vietnam.

"It was hope in the Lord Jesus that kept me alive," he said. "I fed this hope by secretly reading the Scriptures."

Behind the cruel barbed wire, Wilson promised the Lord that he would serve Him if he ever received the opportunity. And the Holy Spirit whispered, "You have opportunities right here!"

Soon, three of his fellow prisoners came to know the Lord.

Camp experiences helped Wilson reflect on the significance of the sufferings of Jesus. And in those reflections, he found refreshment and exhilaration in his own weakness.

"Jesus gave me peace in the midst of my tribulation."[7]

A Few Observations

In today's Scripture reading, Paul points out some trademarks of the active, mature believer: condemned to die in the arena, a spectacle to the whole universe, fools for Christ, weak, dishonored, hungry, thirsty, in rags, brutally treated, homeless, cursed, persecuted, slandered, the scum of the earth, the refuse of the world.

If all this is not happening to me, does it mean I am an inactive, immature believer? Not at all. But if *none* of it *ever* happens to us, it should give us pause, because it is happening daily to brothers and sisters in many other countries. So those of us who enjoy more freedom from persecution are responsible to comfort, strengthen, and encourage those who pay the higher price for their faith.

Food for Thought

"Follow my example," Paul says in 1 Corinthians 11:1, "as I follow the example of Christ." Does Paul mean we need to follow him in his suffering as well as his obedience to Jesus? Consider Paul's exhortation in the light of Jesus' command in Luke 9:23: "If anyone would come after me, he must deny himself and take up his cross daily and follow me."

For Further Study

- 1 John 3:2 assures us that "when he appears, we shall be like him, for we shall see him as he is." God's purpose for each of us is to make us into

the likeness of His Son. Read Isaiah 53:1–10.
- While we are to be transformed into the likeness of Christ, we are also called to be his beautiful and victorious bride. Read Song of Songs, Proverbs 31, and Revelation 21:9–27.

Day 8

GLORIFYING
GOD

We put no stumbling block in anyone's path, so that our ministry will not be discredited. Rather, as servants of God we commend ourselves in every way: in great endurance; in troubles, hardships and distresses; in beatings, imprisonments and riots; in hard work, sleepless nights and hunger; in purity, understanding, patience and kindness; in the Holy Spirit and in sincere love; in truthful speech and in the power of God; with weapons of righteousness in the right hand and in the left; through glory and dishonor, bad report and good report; genuine, yet regarded as impostors; known, yet regarded as unknown; dying, and yet we live on; beaten, and yet not killed; sorrowful, yet always rejoicing; poor, yet making many rich; having nothing, and yet possessing everything.

(2 CORINTHIANS 6:3–10)

Bill Harding, a missionary in Ethiopia, originally shared the following story in *Decision* magazine:

> In 1990, *perestroika*, which had already brought many reforms to Russia and eastern Europe, filtered over to Ethiopia. The Ethiopian government restored freedom of worship, and the underground Church surfaced!
>
> At the Church leader's suggestion, we agreed to use a meadow in front of our home for the first church conference in eight years.
>
> We expected about one thousand people from the underground churches to show up for the gathering. But more than ten thousand men, women, and children—some having walked for two or three days—came from all over southern Ethiopia to join in giving thanks for their new freedom. Never will we forget the singing and the preaching of those four days, often in a deluge of rain.

One night, Grace and I were awakened by a loud clap of thunder and rain pounding on our tin roof. Then we began to hear another sound: voices praising God in song.

With tears in our eyes, Grace and I looked at each other. There were no words to express our emotions as we thought of these dear committed soldiers of Christ, many who had undergone persecution and suffering, praising God in their joy at meeting publicly for Him. Praising God for the rain. Praising God in spite of their discomfort![8]

A Few Observations

Paul learned to be content in good times and in bad. He summarizes this in Philippians 4:11–13:

> I am not saying this because I am in need, for I have learned to be content whatever the circumstances. I know what it is to be in need, and I know what it is to have plenty. I have learned the secret of being content in any and every situation, whether well fed or hungry, whether living in plenty or in want. I can do everything through him who gives me strength.

The key to withstanding persecution is to keep focused on Christ rather than on our suffering. Jesus suffered more than any man on earth. Yet, His life and death brought glory to God and not reproach.

John Foxe recorded the life and death stories of the early martyrs. Speaking of the catacombs, Foxe said,

> There are some 60 catacombs near Rome, in which some 600 miles of galleries have been traced, and these are not all. These galleries are about eight feet high and from three to five feet wide, containing on either side several rows of long, low, horizontal recesses, one above another like berths in a ship. In these the dead bodies were placed and the front closed, either by a single marble slab or several great tiles laid in mortar.
>
> On these slabs or tiles, epitaphs or symbols are engraved or painted. Both pagans and Christians buried their dead in these catacombs. When the Christian graves have been opened, the skeletons tell their own terrible tale. Heads are found severed from the body, ribs and shoulder blades are broken, bones are often calcined from fire. But despite the awful story of persecution that we may read here, the inscriptions breathe forth peace and joy and triumph.
>
> Here are a few: "Here lies Marcia, put to rest in a dream of peace." "Lawrence to his sweetest son, borne away of angels." "Victorious in peace and in Christ." "Being called away, he went in peace." Remember

when reading these inscriptions the story the skeletons tell of persecution, of torture, and of fire.

But the full force of these epitaphs is seen when we contrast them with the pagan epitaphs, such as: "Live for the present hour, since we are sure of nothing else." "I lift my hands against the gods who took me away at the age of twenty though I had done no harm." "Once I was not. Now I am not. I know nothing about it, and it is no concern of mine." "Traveler, curse me now as you pass, for I am in darkness and cannot answer."[9]

Food for Thought

Thanksgiving is a key to contentment, just as taking our blessings for granted is a sure road to discontent. "Be joyful always," Paul instructs the church at Thessalonica, "pray continually; give thanks in all circumstances, for this is God's will for you in Christ Jesus" (1 Thessalonians 5:16–18). Think of any areas in your life in which you are discontent. When was the last time you thanked God for those conditions or situations? Begin now to thank Him. Write yourself notes to remember to continue thanking Him, and see if your discontent doesn't melt away.

For Further Study

Enduring persecution is a state of mind as well as spirit.

- Ephesians 4:23 (KJV) says to be "renewed in the spirit of your mind." ("Now your attitudes and thoughts must all be constantly changing for the better" TLB.) We do this by displacing our worldly thoughts and thought patterns with godly thoughts and thought patterns through reading God's Word and beginning to think His thoughts.
- Paul reveals one of his secrets in Philippians 4:8–9:

  Finally, brothers, whatever is true, whatever is noble, whatever is right, whatever is pure, whatever is lovely, whatever is admirable—if anything is excellent or praiseworthy—think about such things. Whatever you have learned or received or heard from me, or seen in me—put it into practice. And the God of peace will be with you.

- All in all, it is a matter of focus and priority. "But seek first his kingdom and his righteousness, and all these things [food, clothing, shelter] will be given to you as well" (Matthew 6:33).

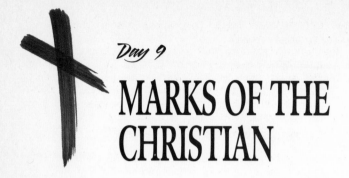

Day 9

MARKS OF THE CHRISTIAN

I bear on my body the marks of Jesus.

(GALATIANS 6:17)

Martha was a young Chinese Christian who was engaged to be married but decided to postpone her marriage for two years to answer God's call to deliver Bibles where they were urgently needed. David Wang shares her story:

> I recall meeting her once in the city of Xian. We had arranged to meet at 9 P.M., but she did not turn up until about 1 A.M. She was delayed because she had been delivering Bibles in a nearby village. But the local commune leaders discovered what she was doing. They beat her up, robbed her, and threw her on a deserted road. It was a miracle that she was able to make it to our appointment.
>
> I noticed something was wrong with Martha. She was thin as a wire, and her face was bloated. I asked, "What is the matter with you? Did they beat you up like this?"
>
> "Oh, no," she said, "I've had this problem for some time now." Then she rolled up her pants to show me legs covered with stings and mosquito bites. As she traveled in the remote countryside of China, often she had to sleep in deserted huts or even out in the fields. She was literally eaten up by bugs and mosquitoes.
>
> "Tomorrow, we must go to a doctor," I urged her.
>
> "No, no," she said, "I have to catch an early train tomorrow to go to Inner Mongolia. Where are the Bibles?" Her only concern was to get the Bibles to Inner Mongolia!
>
> In August 1983, Martha disappeared—as though she had simply vanished into thin air. That was during China's "Anti-Crime Campaign,"

when many people were arrested and executed throughout China. We became concerned for Martha.

Later we got a letter from her through her friends. It was not really a letter—just a little piece of paper. She had been arrested and charged for distributing "superstitious materials" in the People's Republic of China.

The little note read: "I don't know what the penalty will be, but please pray for me." She quoted Paul's words: "Pray for me that whenever I open my mouth, words may be given me so that I will fearlessly make known the mystery of the gospel, for which I am an ambassador in chains" (Ephesians 6:19–20).

A few weeks later, we received word that twenty-four-year-old Martha had been executed. She paid the price.[10]

A Few Observations

A growing number of Christians today carry the marks of Jesus in their flesh. Men, women, and children—imprisoned and tortured for their faith—in Eastern Europe and China, under the Communists; in Latin America and in Islamic countries, at the hands of radical fundamentalists.

But there are other wounds as well. The wounds you can see in the eyes of widows and orphans who have lost husbands and fathers. The wounds in the hearts of children who have had their parents torn from them. The wounds of hunger, need, and ignorance suffered by believers who struggle to survive in Pakistani slums, Egyptian garbage cities, and Sudanese refugee camps.

In the West, the marks are perhaps more difficult to see. Christians are persecuted more by pleasures than prisons. Their enemies are comfort, lust, greed, and apathy. They are blinded by distractions, driven by busyness, and crushed by guilt.

Food for Thought

Is it harder to grow as a Christian in America or Europe or in countries like China and Cuba, which openly persecute believers? If so, why?

For Further Study

Christians bear two kinds of marks: of suffering and of ownership.

- Exodus 21:5–6 describes a slave who is set free but loves his master too much to leave. "But if the servant declares, 'I love my master and my wife and children and do not want to go free,' then his master must take him

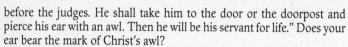

before the judges. He shall take him to the door or the doorpost and pierce his ear with an awl. Then he will be his servant for life." Does your ear bear the mark of Christ's awl?

- Ezekiel 9 speaks of the purification of the remnant of Israel, how God commanded that a mark be placed on the forehead of everyone who mourned and wept over the abominations that were done in that nation. Everyone without that mark would be put to the sword.

- The things that mark an apostle—patience, signs, wonders, and mighty deeds—are listed in 2 Corinthians 12:12.

- And, of course, there is the contrary mark of Satan in the end times prophesy of Revelation 13:16, the mark that is to be placed on the right hand or forehead of every person in order to buy or sell.

- The wicked man, according to Job 15:22, is marked for the sword.

- And Ephesians 1:13 says we were marked with a seal, the promised Holy Spirit, when we believed in Jesus.

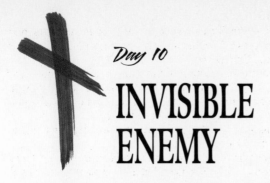

Day 10

INVISIBLE ENEMY

For our struggle is not against flesh and blood, but against the rulers, against the authorities, against the powers of this dark world and against the spiritual forces of evil in the heavenly realms.

(EPHESIANS 6:12)

Kefa Sempangi, as pastor of the large Redeemed Church of Uganda, faced many death threats and attempts on his life before ultimately escaping the country. Easter Sunday 1973 was his first serious brush with death at the hands of the secret police—Idi Amin's Nubian assassins. After an all-day worship service, Pastor Sempangi went to the vestry to change clothes—too exhausted to notice the five strangers following him. In his book *A Distant Grief*, Sempangi reveals what followed.

"We are going to kill you," said the leader as the men pointed their rifles at Sempangi's face. "If you have something to say, say it before you die."

"I am a dead man already," Sempangi heard himself saying. "My life is dead in Christ. It is your lives that are in danger; you are dead in your sins. I will pray to God that after you have killed me, He will spare you from eternal destruction."

The leader lowered his gun and motioned to the others to do the same.

"Will you pray for us now?" he asked.

"Yes," Sempangi answered.

Together they lowered their heads.

"Father in heaven . . . you have forgiven men in the past, forgive these men also. Do not let them perish in their sins but bring them unto yourself."

The tall leader spoke first.

"You have helped us," he said, "and we will help you. We will speak to the rest of our company. Do not fear for your life. It is in our hands, and you will be protected."[11]

A Few Observations

The Jews were not the enemies of the church, nor were the Romans, Papists, or Communists. And our enemies today are not governments, cults, secret police, or religious groups.

Yes, men wield the swords and turn the torture racks and mock and jeer. But they are servants, even as we are servants. The war is, and has always been, waged by the kingdom of this world against the kingdom of God and His Christ.

This is why the believer's most powerful weapon is prayer, not politics. Prayer defeats the real, unseen enemies, while politics are effective only against men and ideas.

Prayer crosses borders that are closed to Christians and the Gospel. Prayer looses the bonds of prisoners. Prayer shines light into the darkness of lies and false religion. Prayer opens the way for God to move where man cannot. It succeeds where all of our efforts fail.

Prayer releases the miracles that defied the flames for the Hebrew children, that shut the mouths of the lions, and that have enabled ordinary people to perform extraordinary feats and endure extraordinary suffering.

Food for Thought

What prayers has God answered in your life? What testimonies do you have of God's faithfulness? Thus armed and strengthened in your faith, ask the Holy Spirit to burden your heart for your persecuted brethren and to drive you to your knees in prayer for them.

For Further Study

- Read the description in Daniel 9 and 10 of the heavenly battle between the principality over Persia and the angel sent by God to answer Daniel's prayers for Israel.
- God delivered Hezekiah from the hands of Sennacherib because of prayer—2 Kings 19:19–20.
- God defeated the enemies of Jehoshaphat in answer to prayer—2 Chronicles 18:31.

- Elizabeth became pregnant with John the Baptist as the result of prayer—Luke 1:13.
- Even Pentecost was the result of prayer—Acts 4:31.

Suggested Activity

Many prayers have been answered that seem impossible to man. When one person commits to pray for a particular need for forty straight days, miracles can happen. Try this by praying for forty days for the salvation of those you love or those who persecute you.

Day 11

BLESSED ASSURANCE

Brothers, I do not consider myself yet to have taken hold of it. But one thing I do: Forgetting what is behind and straining toward what is ahead, I press on toward the goal to win the prize for which God has called me heavenward in Christ Jesus. . . . But our citizenship is in heaven. And we eagerly await a Savior from there, the Lord Jesus Christ, who, by the power that enables him to bring everything under his control, will transform our lowly bodies so that they will be like his glorious body.

(PHILIPPIANS 3:13–14, 20–21)

Just before he was executed by the Communists, a Romanian Christian prisoner wrote a prayer:

> Lord, I look forward to the great day I see you and your family in heaven. I look forward to seeing the great evangelists standing before you. I look forward to the day I see all the missionaries coming home rejoicing with their sheaves. I look forward to hearing all the great singers of the world praising you. I look forward to seeing the great preachers of the ages standing before you. But Lord, I have one special request. When that day comes, allow me to be there in the clothing of a prisoner. I want to praise you throughout eternity in my prisoner's clothes to always remind me that I was a prisoner for you.[12]

A Few Observations

In the martial arts, to break a wooden board or stone block with your hand, you focus all of your attention on a point *beyond* the object. Your goal is to reach that point. Whatever is in the way, whether board or block, is of no consequence.

So, too, persecuted Christians gain unbelievable strength from the blessed assurance of eternal life. Of life beyond pain and suffering. Of life with Jesus, their heart's desire.

Even at the point of death, there is joy for the believer, just as there was for the good thief at Calvary. To each of us, as our suffering draws to an end, Jesus says, "I tell you the truth, today you will be with me in paradise" (Luke 23:43).

Food for Thought

Write down as many things as you can imagine that will be different in heaven. What do you suffer in this life that you will no longer suffer in the next? What do you think heaven will be like?

For Further Study

- In 2 Corinthians 5:6–8, Paul says he would rather be with the Lord than on earth. And again, in Philippians 1:21–24, Paul explains that death, to him, is preferable to this life, but that it is more profitable for the church if he remains for a season.
- Romans 8:18–19 says present suffering cannot even be compared to future glory, and it reveals that even creation longs for the day that God will resurrect his children and there will be a new heaven and a new earth.
- Read Isaiah 35, 2 Peter 3:13, and Revelation 21:1–6.

REMEMBER MY BONDS

My fellow prisoner Aristarchus sends you his greetings, as does Mark, the cousin of Barnabas. (You have received instructions about him; if he comes to you, welcome him.) Jesus, who is called Justus, also sends greetings. These are the only Jews among my fellow workers for the kingdom of God, and they have proved a comfort to me. Epaphras, who is one of you and a servant of Christ Jesus, sends greetings. He is always wrestling in prayer for you, that you may stand firm in all the will of God, mature and fully assured. I vouch for him that he is working hard for you and for those at Laodicea and Hierapolis. Our dear friend Luke, the doctor, and Demas send greetings. . . . I, Paul, write this greeting in my own hand. Remember my chains. . . .

(COLOSSIANS 4:10–14, 18)

Christians in the suffering church visit brothers and sisters in prison regularly. One reason is for the encouragement they bring.

Another is that they can bring much-needed gifts of food. There are numerous reports of how these visiting Christians stand outside the camp or prison after their short visit and sing at the top of their lungs.

Here is one such song translated from Chinese into English:

I'm a little bird in a cage,
away from the trees, flowers and fields.
To be in bonds for you, Lord,
how glad I am to sing
and pour out my heart to You all day.
You like to hold my wings that like to fly.
Listen to the songs that I have to sing.
Your great love constrains me;

I'll be your love slave who will never run away.
Who will understand the bitterness of prison life?
But the love of the Lord can make it sweet;
Oh Lord, I love the road You have prepared for me.
May the whole creation praise your wonderful deeds.

The Christian prisoner for whom this was sung stood on the balcony and wept, touched beyond measure.[13]

A Few Observations

Paul makes it a point in his letters to the churches to give honor to those who minister with him and help him in his work, especially during the time he spent in prison before he was martyred.

He says they are a comfort to him. And he praises their love, labors, and prayers for the church.

"Rejoice with those who rejoice," Paul instructs us in Romans 12:15, "mourn with those who mourn." And in Luke 4:18, Jesus quotes Isaiah 61, saying that God sent Him "to preach good news to the poor . . . to proclaim freedom for the prisoners and recovery of sight for the blind, to release the oppressed, to proclaim the year of the Lord's favor."

Let us all, at every opportunity, minister to our persecuted brothers and sisters—through our prayers, by going to them with words of comfort and encouragement, and by bringing them the nourishment of God's Word.

Food for Thought

Paul closes his greetings with a plea. "Remember my chains." Was he asking for more help and comfort? Was he trying to encourage the believers? If so, how? What can be learned from the chains of prisoners? Refer to some of the Scriptures below.

For Further Study

- What lesson can be learned from the chains in the account of Paul and Silas in Acts 16?
- What do you think Paul meant in Acts 26:29 when he told King Agrippa, "I pray God that not only you but all who are listening to me today may become what I am, except for these chains"?
- What lesson is there for us in 2 Timothy 1:16, where Paul praised Onesiphorus who "often refreshed me and was not ashamed of my chains,"

and in his intercession on behalf of the escaped slave Onesimus "who became my son while I was in chains"? (Philemon 1:10).

Suggested Activity

Memorize Isaiah 35:4–10. It describes a world without sin or pain. By memorizing it, you will always be ready to ease the suffering of a brother or sister with words of comfort.

Day 13

STAND FIRM

We sent Timothy, who is our brother and God's fellow worker in spreading the gospel of Christ, to strengthen and encourage you in your faith, so that no one would be unsettled by these trials. You know quite well that we were destined for them. In fact, when we were with you, we kept telling you that we would be persecuted. And it turned out that way, as you well know. For this reason, when I could stand it no longer, I sent to find out about your faith. I was afraid that in some way the tempter might have tempted you and our efforts might have been useless.

(1 Thessalonians 3:2–5)

A Christian medical doctor in China shares an experience when he refused to bow down or *kowtow* (touch one's forehead to the ground as an expression of respect or submission) to an image of Mao because of his love for Jesus. After severe beatings failed to influence him, the authorities resorted to a more subtle strategy by getting his whole family to stand around him and weep. Hear the story in his own words:

> I had seven children, as well as my wife, all surrounding me and weeping. Crying bitterly, my wife said to me, "If you don't kowtow you will surely die and then what will we do?" For three days they stood around me weeping until my wife's eyes were dreadfully swollen.
>
> "After you have died, what will happen to these children? Please, for the sake of your family, just kowtow."
>
> They cried and cried. I really did not know what to do. I felt that I had no more strength so I prayed, "Lord I have no strength left, what must I do?"
>
> On the third day, the Lord's word came, "If you do not love Me more

than your own parents, wife, children, brothers and sisters, or even your own life, you cannot be my disciple" (Luke 14:26).

Hallelujah! There is no word of the Lord that is without power. The Lord through His Word filled me with the life and power of God.

I said to my wife, "Stop crying. It's no use your crying. I am the Lord's disciple. For the Lord's sake, I am ready to die!"

When it came to my attending "morning orders" they told me to kowtow, but I said I was a Christian and even if they beat me to death, I still would not worship an image.

They replied, "If you do not kowtow today, we shall beat you to death and then we shall see in whose hand is the power and authority."

Of course I would not kowtow and so they started with their beating. My Lord did not leave me but caused me to taste something of what He knew when beaten in Pilate's court. No one sympathized with our Lord then. He gave His life for us. Is there anything we will not give for Him?

They beat me to the ground and then dragged me off with a rope to the "cowshed" where they bound me and hung me up to be beaten until I was senseless. They then heated irons in the fire and poked at my face.

I only vaguely heard the sizzling sound, but I felt no pain. Previously I had never understood the words, "My heart melted like wax within me." When the Lord was crucified, His heart was melted like wax, and now I had tasted this and understood.

Someone lifted my eyelids and looked at my eyes. "Quick, let him down, his pupils are dilated, he's dead." I heard this voice and knew that the Lord had not forsaken me.

Then the day came when the chief called me and said, "You had better consider your situation carefully. If you want to live, you must kowtow. Otherwise it will mean certain death for you. Tonight we will make you eat the "steel bean" (bullet); you will be executed! This is your very last opportunity!" And so he sent me back to think it over.

There was, however, no need for me to think it over; I was ready for the bullet. But the night passed without my being called.

Next day, I saw that outside folk were running hither and thither and I wondered whatever had happened to cause such alarm. Later I was to learn that immediately after I had left the office, black swellings appeared on the chief's legs, and it was frightfully painful. Because he was the chief, all the doctors in the hospital were rushed to his side to give him aid. But the black spots spread very quickly and, within twenty-four hours, he was dead.

No wonder I had not been called.[14]

A Few Observations

None of us wants to believe we would deny Christ under pressure. But few in the West have experienced the kind of pressure suffered by Christians in many other countries today. Paul was very concerned about it, as he makes clear in his letter to the church in Thessalonica.

Jesus himself warned the disciples about what was to come. "Then you will be handed over to be persecuted and put to death, and you will be hated by all nations because of me. At that time many will turn away from the faith and will betray and hate each other, and many false prophets will appear and deceive many people. Because of the increase of wickedness, the love of most will grow cold" (Matthew 24:9–12).

Although Christians in the West are not yet imprisoned and martyred for their faith, they are in every other part of the world. Here in the West, however, iniquity does indeed abound, and many believers are turning from the path to follow the world's ways—lying to make a sale or keep a client, cheating on taxes, using inferior materials to make greater profits, bribing, stealing, and manipulating.

The writer of Hebrews might have been speaking to Western believers today when he wrote, "In your struggle against sin, you have not yet resisted to the point of shedding your blood" (Hebrews 12:4).

Food for Thought

We will never know for certain what we would do under persecution until we face it. But considering some issues in advance can help reveal what is currently in our hearts. For example, if you live in a country where tithes and alms are tax-deductible, would you continue to give if they were not? What do you think you would do if it became illegal in your country to own a Bible? What would you do if your government began to shut down all the churches?

For Further Study

- Read the parable of the sower in Matthew 13:1–23, especially focusing on verses 20–21.
- Matthew 26:56 records the apostles' response to the threat of persecution.
- Peter's denial, recorded in all four of the gospels, demonstrates how even those closest to Jesus can momentarily lose their focus and respond in the flesh. It should also give us compassion for those who fail under pres-

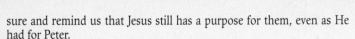

sure and remind us that Jesus still has a purpose for them, even as He had for Peter.

- 2 Timothy 4:9–16 shows us that, as the day of Paul's execution drew nearer, even his closest friends abandoned him.

Day 14

PREVAILING PRAYER

Finally, brothers, pray for us that the message of the Lord may spread rapidly and be honored, just as it was with you. And pray that we may be delivered from wicked and evil men, for not everyone has faith.

(2 THESSALONIANS 3:1–2)

A missionary on furlough shared this story while visiting his home church in Michigan:

> While serving at a small field hospital in Africa, every two weeks I traveled by bicycle through the jungle to a nearby city for supplies. This was a journey of two days and required camping overnight at the halfway point.
>
> On one of these journeys, I arrived in the city where I planned to collect money from a bank, purchase medicine and supplies, and then begin my two-day journey back to the field hospital.
>
> Upon arrival in the city, I observed two men fighting, one of whom had been seriously injured. I treated him for his injuries and at the same time witnessed to him about the Lord Jesus Christ. I then traveled two days, camped overnight, and arrived home without incident.
>
> Two weeks later I repeated my journey.
>
> Upon arriving in the city, I was approached by the young man I had treated. He told me that he had known I carried money and medicine.
>
> "Some friends and I followed you into the jungle, knowing you would camp overnight," he said. "We planned to kill you and take your money and drugs. But just as we were about to move into your camp, we saw that you were surrounded by twenty-six armed guards."
>
> At this I laughed and said that I was certainly all alone out in that jungle campsite.

The young man pressed the point, however, and said, "No sir, I was not the only person to see the guards. My five friends also saw them, and we all counted them. It was because of those guards that we were afraid and left you alone."

At this point in the sermon, one of the men in the congregation jumped to his feet and interrupted the missionary and asked if he could tell him the exact day that this happened. The missionary told the congregation the date, and the man who interrupted told him this story:

"On the night of your incident in Africa, it was morning here and I was preparing to go play golf . . . when I felt the urge to pray for you. In fact, the urging of the Lord was so strong, I called men in this church to meet with me here in the sanctuary to pray for you. Would all of those men who met with me on that day stand up?"

The men who had met together to pray that day stood up. The missionary wasn't concerned with who they were—he was too busy counting how many men he saw.

There were twenty-six.[15]

A Few Observations

Too much cannot be said about the importance of prayer. A few days ago, we saw that the Christian's battle on earth is a spiritual one, and prayer is his most effective weapon.

That's why there is so much opposition to prayer: "I've no time to pray." "I've no place to pray." "I don't know what to pray." "I don't know where to begin." "I pray but I don't see results."

But, as Oswald Chambers noted, "The reason for intercession is not that God answers prayer, but that God tells us to pray."[16]

For the Christian, prayer is not an option. It's a command. "Pray for those who persecute you," Jesus says (Matthew 5:44). "Pray that you will not fall into temptation," He says in Luke 22:40. Paul, in Ephesians 6:18, says we are to "pray in the Spirit on all occasions with all kinds of prayers and requests. With this in mind, be alert and always keep on praying for all the saints."

"Pray for us, too," Paul begged, "that God may open a door for our message, so that we may proclaim the mystery of Christ, for which I am in chains" (Colossians 4:3). And we saw earlier (Day 8) that God's expressed will for each of us is that we "pray continually" (1 Thessalonians 5:17).

Food for Thought

What difficulties do you have in maintaining a consistent prayer life? What suggestions can you find in Scripture and from personal experience for overcoming these difficulties?

For Further Study

"But seek first his kingdom and his righteousness," Jesus said, "and all these things will be given to you as well" (Matthew 6:33). If this is true, then the solution to every problem on earth will be found in the presence of God. Jesus himself prayed before every critical point in His life:

- He prayed and fasted every day for over a month before beginning His public ministry (Matthew 4).
- He prayed before He selected His disciples (Luke 6:12).
- Before walking on the waters of Galilee, He had been praying (Matthew 14:22–25).
- He was praying before the Transfiguration (Luke 9:28–29).
- In John 17, Jesus prayed for His disciples, for us, and for the lost.
- And He went off alone to pray before His betrayal and crucifixion (Matthew 26:36).
- Read also Exodus 33:7–11 to learn about the Tent of Meeting where Moses and Joshua went to meet with the Lord. (Note that even when Moses left the tent, Joshua stayed. This habitual intimacy with God would be critical in the days after the death of Moses.)

Recommended Reading

The subject of prayer is so important that Open Doors encourages its leaders to read several additional books, including:

Power through Prayer, E. M. Bounds, 1992, Baker Book House, Grand Rapids, Mich.

No Easy Road, Dick Eastman, 1973, Baker Book House, Grand Rapids, Mich.

The Practice of the Presence of God, Brother Lawrence, 1989 (paperback edition), Fleming H. Revell Co., a division of Baker Book House, Grand Rapids, Mich.

Shaping History Through Prayer and Fasting, Derek Prince, 1994 (paperback edition), Whitaker House, Springdale, Pa.

God's Chosen Fast, Arthur Wallis, 1986, Christian Literature Crusade, Ft. Washington, Pa.

Rees Howells, Intercessor, Norman Grubb, 1988, Christian Literature Crusade, Ft. Washington, Pa.

Day 15

LORD, SEND LEADERS!

Here is a trustworthy saying: If anyone sets his heart on being an overseer, he desires a noble task.

(1 TIMOTHY 3:1)

An instructor from the West spent time in China with young leaders who needed training. The following is an excerpt from his report:

> Not surprisingly, these leaders tended to be young and single. Who else would have the energy? It does take its toll on them, however. Some confided that they got depressed. One young man shared very openly about his longing to be married: "I just don't want to be lonely anymore."
>
> Gradually, I realized that although their pressures are very different from ours, their problems are very similar. They struggle with loneliness and fear, intimacy issues, and depression.
>
> The seeping in of materialism and superstitions from the wider culture troubles their churches. Often their leaders are power-hungry, wishing to build empires of control rather than a kingdom of empowered saints. I learned this after teaching how the Corinthians were fragmented through following Peter, Apollos, or Paul. That teaching seemed to hit home.
>
> All the time I struggled with a great sense of unworthiness. Who am I to teach fifty men and women who had been in jail, who were on the run for God, having "nowhere to lay their heads"?
>
> "I don't feel equipped to teach you!" I told them.
>
> They looked shocked. "But you have an education," they said. "You have the knowledge we need. We want to know more about the Bible, about its background, the issues and themes, the way it all hangs together."

I began to repent of my attitude toward biblical scholars, whom I had tended to dismiss as a bunch of useless intellectuals. I was keenly aware that I was now dependent upon their material. I could not have introduced these young people to Corinthians without the work of F. F. Bruce, Gordon Fee, and others.

We are so fortunate to have seminaries, Bible colleges, libraries, and software with many different translations. I came back determined to use all that to the best of my ability, seeing it all as a wonderful gift of God.

As I left them, I wept because I had to return to a world where God was not taken half as seriously as He was here. I wept to return to a church that won't listen to a sermon that doesn't glisten with clever illustrations. I wept to return to a world of unread Bibles and dry eyes.

I wept for those who would consider me mad to rise at 4:30 A.M. for prayer.

And I wept because I wanted to stay with those fifty teachers and learn to love God as they did.[17]

A Few Observations

"Smite the shepherd," warns Zechariah 13:7 (KJV), "and the sheep shall be scattered."

Trained leaders are one of the most vital needs of the persecuted church. Without them, the church cannot grow, and weak, young sheep are devoured by cults and heresies.

In some nations that are hostile to the Gospel, thousands of believers are led by young pastors who are themselves new in the Lord. Some of these congregations have only a few Bibles. As such, they are easy targets for the Evil One. Without shepherds, many fall amid persecution.

One of the chief missions of Open Doors is to provide leadership training in so-called closed countries. Teachers take great personal risks to cross hostile borders and often spend many sleepless nights instructing eager candidates who also risk their freedom—even their lives—to attend.

Food for Thought

What part have trained ministers of the Gospel played in your life? What would your life be like today without their input?

For Further Study

- Read all of 1 Timothy 3 for Paul's qualifications for pastors, elders, and deacons.

- Jeremiah 23:2 and 50:6 speak of God's judgment against false shepherds.
- God spoke to the prophet Ezekiel about pastors who abuse their sheep for selfish gain (Ezekiel 34:2–3).
- But Jeremiah 3:15 and 23:4 tells us that God also promised that He would give His people shepherds after His own heart who will care for the church and protect it.
- Ephesians 4:11–13 says that God gave us apostles, prophets, evangelists, and teachers—as well as pastors—"to prepare God's people for works of service, so that the body of Christ may be built up until we all reach unity in the faith and in the knowledge of the Son of God and become mature, attaining to the whole measure of the fullness of Christ."

Suggested Activity

Form your own prayer group with other church members or friends. Commit yourselves to pray ten minutes a day for those who suffer for a lifetime.

Day 16

HE DELIVERED ME

You, however, know all about my teaching, my way of life, my purpose, faith, patience, love, endurance, persecutions, sufferings—what kinds of things happened to me in Antioch, Iconium and Lystra, the persecutions I endured. Yet the Lord rescued me from all of them.

(2 TIMOTHY 3:10–11)

A young woman was dragged roughly to the basement of her house by her two elder brothers. She was pushed to the wall while her older brother held a loaded gun to her mouth and whispered, "Deny Jesus, and you will live; return to Islam, and you shall not die."

Frightened, the woman looked from one brother to the next. She knew that, as a new believer, she had brought great shame to her family. According to the religious custom, her brothers had been given the task and the authority to kill her.

Months earlier, her family had disowned her and forced her to leave her home. Then, suddenly, her family invited her back. They showered her with gifts and hospitality. The whole family, including her father, seemed to have forgiven her for her betrayal of Islam.

Then, late one evening, her father came to speak with her.

"If you love me and your family, you must leave your craziness and return to Islam. You must stop reading your Bible, and you must deny Jesus. If not, you leave me no choice. You must decide now."

Now she stood before her brothers.

"You cannot kill me," she said softly. "Jesus has taken my sin and has promised that I will live forever. He has prepared a place for me in heaven. You will not kill me, for I now have eternal life."

Her brothers shook with anger. The oldest brother squeezed the trigger of the gun.

Nothing happened.

Again he pulled the trigger. Six times he tried to fire the gun, but nothing happened. Enraged, they grabbed her and took her to the front gate of the house.

"Leave now, and never return here again. You are dead to us!"

Several years later, both her brothers and several members of her family found faith in the Lord Jesus.[18]

A Few Observations

Among the martyrs during the reign of England's Queen Mary were bishops Ridley and Latimer. They were burned at the stake at Oxford. Despite the flames, however, the Lord delivered them:

> The place of death was on the north side of the town, opposite Baliol College. . . . When they came to the stake, Mr. Ridley embraced Latimer fervently and bid him: "Be of good heart, brother, for God will either assuage the fury of the flame, or else strengthen us to abide it. . . ." A lighted [stick] was now laid at Dr. Ridley's feet, which caused Mr. Latimer to say: "Be of good cheer, Ridley; and play the man. We shall this day, by God's grace, light up such a candle in England, as I trust, will never be put out."
>
> When Dr. Ridley saw the fire flaming up toward him, he cried with a wonderful loud voice, "Lord, Lord, receive my spirit." Master Latimer, crying as vehemently on the other side, "O Father of heaven, receive my soul!" received the flame as it were embracing of it. After that he had stroked his face with his hands, and as it were, bathed them a little in the fire, he soon died (as it appeareth) with very little pain or none.[19]

Food for Thought

Not every martyr dies without pain. But Jesus promises that He will never leave nor forsake us (Hebrews 13:5). "And surely I will be with you always," He said, "to the very end of the age" (Matthew 28:20). Though we may be thrown into the flames, He has demonstrated that we will never go in alone (Daniel 3). How has God delivered you from death or injury, wrong choices, or temptation? Have you ever sensed His presence as you were going through a severe trial?

For Further Study

- Read God's promise of deliverance in Job 5:19.
- God will always deliver us from every temptation; we are assured of this in 1 Corinthians 10:13.
- See also 2 Timothy 4:18; 2 Peter 2:9; 2 Samuel 22:2; Isaiah 46:4; Daniel 6:27; and 2 Corinthians 1:10.

Day 17

SUBMITTED TO RULERS

Remind the people to be subject to rulers and authorities, to be obedient, to be ready to do whatever is good, to slander no one, to be peaceable and considerate, and to show true humility toward all men.

(Titus 3:1–2)

Mikhail Khorev, a very effective evangelist in Russia, spent many years in prison for his continued public ministry. On one occasion, his family was refused visiting rights and sent home.

When the prison guard was taunting him about it, he replied, "I would like to tell you that my God is fulfilling His plans through you and will use you for our blessing. I love my family very much, and being together with them means a lot to me. But if it brings more honor to the Lord for us to part rather than be together, then why should I insist on seeing them?

"If His name is glorified more through my being in prison than through my being at liberty, then I tell you that there is no greater joy for me than to die on this prison bunk as a prisoner, as my father did and as many of my brothers in the faith have done."

Mikhail is also quoted as saying, "I have to admit to you that prison is a very useful school for our education and for the testing of the genuineness of our faith. . . . I'm grateful to the Lord for this school and for His leading."[20]

A Few Observations

On Day 5, we saw how Peter and John were forced to choose between obeying God or man. They chose God. Nevertheless, even though the religious rulers were wrong in what they were doing, the authority they wielded

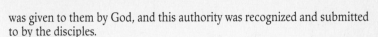

was given to them by God, and this authority was recognized and submitted to by the disciples.

Like millions of our brothers and sisters in the world today, Peter and John allowed themselves to be taken to prison—just as Jesus submitted Himself to arrest, judgment, and execution.

"Do you refuse to speak to me?" Pilate said. "Don't you realize I have power either to free you or to crucify you?" Jesus answered, "You would have no power over me if it were not given to you from above. Therefore the one who handed me over to you is guilty of a greater sin." (John 19:10–11).

Whether our rulers be righteous or not, God commands His people to submit to the authorities over them (Romans 13:1) and to love them and pray for them (Matthew 5:44).

Food for Thought

Traditionally, most of the church has strenuously opposed pornography, homosexuality, and abortion. Has the church spoken of the government and other leaders who allow these sins with respect, or disrespect? Loved or hated them? Prayed for or against them? What is the biblical way to protest and oppose unrighteousness?

For Further Study

- Read Romans 13:5.
- In the same way, we are to submit to the leaders God has set up in our churches (Hebrews 13:17).
- Likewise, we are to submit to to our employers (1 Peter 2:18–19).

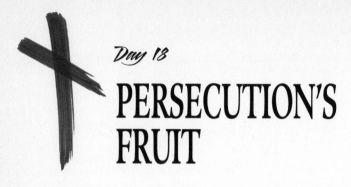

Day 18

PERSECUTION'S FRUIT

I appeal to you for my son Onesimus, who became my son while I was in chains.
(PHILEMON 1:10)

Open Doors' founder, Brother Andrew, shares a testimony about a Christian prisoner named Sylvador Ali Ahmad in Sudan. Ahmad was a respected Muslim leader and a brilliant scholar.

While studying for his doctorate in comparative religions, he began reading the New Testament and ultimately gave his life to Jesus.

Then, in 1991, *Shari'a*, [law of Islam] became the law of the land in Sudan. Ahmad was called in for questioning. When he admitted to being a Christian, he was arrested, chained, and thrown into solitary confinement.

The first night in prison, the authorities tried to kill him. Unexplainably, however, they could find no petrol for their car to drive him to the place of execution.

The next day he was to be arraigned before the Islamic High Court. A lawyer friend urged him to renounce his faith publicly and keep it secretly in his heart. Ahmad refused.

"Jesus is my only defense," he said. "I cannot deny Him."

Ahmad was sentenced to six months in prison, stripped of his military rank, and fired from his teaching position. His wife had already divorced him. He also lost his four children, his car, his house, and his bank account. If at the end of his sentence he still refused to return to Islam, the judges said, he would spend six more months behind bars.

Ahmad organized small Bible studies and prayer groups throughout Omdurman Prison.

"By the end of three months," he said, "there were 305 known Christians in our prison, at least seven from Muslim background."

Labeling him "a very dangerous man," the prison *imam* [teacher] had him transferred to Gerif Prison, a work facility in east Khartoum. There Ahmad continued to spread the Gospel.

In this prison, Ahmad and seven other Christians began meeting together. After a week, fifty gathered around a tree in the prison courtyard. Two months later, there were 115 believers, growing bolder and experiencing miraculous answers to their prayers.

One night, the guards threw Ahmad into a truck with orders to drown him in the Nile. But as the truck neared the river, it mysteriously stopped. Terrified, the guards and driver refused the officer's orders to kill Ahmad. Soon afterward, he was released.

"When so many were getting converted around me in the prison," he explains, "they must have decided it was better for me to be outside!"[21]

A Few Observations

Onesimus was a runaway slave who belonged to a believer named Philemon (whom Paul addresses as one who himself was won to Christ through Paul and is therefore indebted to him).

While serving Paul in prison, Onesimus gave his life to the Lord, repented of escaping from his master, and agreed to return and make restitution. Paul's letter precedes Onesimus and pleads for mercy and forgiveness from Philemon.

Only God knows how many people have seen the Truth in the light of the martyrs' flames. Only He knows how many souls have been set free by the labors of imprisoned believers. There are even many testimonies of guards and tormentors won to Christ as they tortured His children.

Pray for those in prison. Not only that they may be released and that God would care for and comfort their families, but that they would leave behind bars a strong, thriving church that would set many more prisoners free.

Food for Thought

In Romans 8:28, Paul assures believers, "We know that in all things God works for the good of those who love him, who have been called according to his purpose." Can that include persecution? Temptation? Imprisonment and death? What good other than converted souls can come from these forms of persecution? How can this promise help us pray more effectively for our persecuted brethren?

For Further Study

- David sinned with Bathsheba, and they lost their son. But God raised up the world's Messiah from their descendants (2 Samuel 11; Matthew 1:6).
- Moses sinned (Numbers 20:8–12) and was forbidden to enter the Promised Land. Yet God used Moses to bring Israel out of captivity and buried him with His own hands at the foot of Mount Nebo (Deuteronomy 34:6). And, thousands of years later, Moses appeared glorified along with Elijah and Jesus on the Mount of Transfiguration (Mark 9:2–9).
- Acts 8–9 tell us that the new church was persecuted and scattered following Stephen's martyrdom. But we also see much good resulting from it, including healings and conversions in Samaria and the conversions of an important Ethiopian official and a religious zealot named Saul.

Suggested Activity

Read through the New Testament and highlight every apostolic prayer that you find (e.g., Romans 10:1–4, 15:5–6, 13; 2 Corinthians 13:14; 1 Thessalonians 3:11, 5:23). Pray these back to God when you pray for the suffering church in the assurance that these biblical prayers will be heard and answered.

Day 19

CALLED TO PERSEVERE

Remember those earlier days after you had received the light, when you stood your ground in a great contest in the face of suffering. Sometimes you were publicly exposed to insult and persecution; at other times you stood side by side with those who were so treated. You sympathized with those in prison and joyfully accepted the confiscation of your property, because you knew that you yourselves had better and lasting possessions. So do not throw away your confidence; it will be richly rewarded. You need to persevere so that when you have done the will of God, you will receive what he has promised.

(HEBREWS 10:32–36)

Sister Pasqualita suffered severe persecution in her small town in the very southern part of Mexico after she became an evangelical. Other Christians had been driven from the town.

One night, an angry mob surrounded her grass-roofed home and set it ablaze. As she opened the door, gunfire erupted.

"I thank the Lord that only twenty-one ammunition bits (bullets) touched me," she said.

Sister Pasqualita was shot all over her body, even in the neck. She was still able to run, until she fell into a hole. Her persecutors couldn't see her there in the dark.

She was losing blood rapidly. Then some townsfolk who had heard her testimony rescued her and took her to a clinic in a nearby town.

She survived, but three other family members in the house were murdered.

Sister Pasqualita complained to the Lord, saying, "Lord, why, now that I've given you my life and my family, am I suffering this way?"

The Lord reminded her of a song that she used to sing often: "I have decided to follow Jesus; no turning back."

"Then I understood that when I decided to follow Jesus," she recalls, "it was in the midst of any situation, any persecution. My life now belonged to Him. I gained strength in that song. I am preaching again and I am encouraging the rest of the believers that when we decide to follow Jesus, there is no turning back."[22]

A Few Observations

Sister Pasqualita's story highlights what is happening to the persecuted church in countries all over the world today. Believers in China and Sudan, throughout Latin America, and in Islamic countries have their homes and goods confiscated by the government or destroyed by angry mobs.

Yet they rejoice.

Many of us in the West, although we have not yet suffered to this degree, suffered mocking and estrangement from friends and family members when we came to Christ.

But the writer of Hebrews warns that it is possible to drift away from the affection for the Lord that once burned in our hearts and enabled us to rejoice in the midst of that suffering.

Let us pray for one another as Jesus prayed for Peter in Luke 22:31, that we might not fall into temptation and allow our affection for Christ to grow cold.

Food for Thought

Hebrews speaks of the saints standing "side by side with those who were so treated." This describes an obligation of every Christian. Believers, especially in the relatively free West, are to become the companions of persecuted believers; we are to do whatever we can to strengthen and encourage them and meet their physical needs.

How has the companionship of fellow believers helped you through difficult times? How have your needs been met by God through your brothers and sisters? In what ways can you be a *companion* to persecuted believers in other countries?

For Further Study

- Jesus encourages us in Matthew 25:35–46 to be a companion to those in need, saying that as we are their companion, we are also His.

- Paul speaks as a member of the persecuted church in Philippians 4:10–19, listing his needs and expressing his deep appreciation for the companionship of the believers in Philippi.
- Paul closes his letter to the church in Colosse with affectionate greetings from his faithful companions (Colossians 4:10–14).
- Companionship with the persecuted church can be wearisome because of the great and pressing needs. But Paul encourages believers, in Galatians 6:9, not to give up.

Day 20

JOYFUL TRIALS

Consider it pure joy, my brothers, whenever you face trials of many kinds, because you know that the testing of your faith develops perseverance. Perseverance must finish its work so that you may be mature and complete, not lacking anything.

(JAMES 1:2–4)

J. J. Andrews is an elderly Lutheran pastor friend in Rangoon, Burma (now Yangon, Myanmar) with a great heart for ministry.

Several years ago his daughter died of viral hepatitis. Two months later his wife passed away from a broken heart. And six months after that, one of his sons died suddenly.

Brother J. J. was crushed.

"I felt like Job," he recalls, "only no one visited me."

Ver Enriquez, a young Filipino staff member of Open Doors in Bangkok, Thailand, heard about this situation. He made a special trip just to visit Brother J. J. and to encourage him.

"Thank you for coming in my darkest hour," J. J. told him.

If you visit Brother J. J. today, you will see his young grandchildren laughing and playing around his home. He will smile and share unforgettable lessons with you.

"God rewarded me for my perseverance," he will tell you, "and healed my broken heart!"[23]

A Few Observations

Paul and Silas understood joyful trials. Acts 16:22–23 says they were arrested, stripped, and beaten. Then they were thrown into a dungeon and their feet made fast in wooden stocks.

Their response: "About midnight Paul and Silas were praying and singing hymns to God" (v. 25).

We have only to read the rest of the book of Acts to see how this exercise of patience in persecution strengthened them for the trials ahead.

Paul and Silas understood the value of patience. So did Oswald Chambers:

> God takes the saints like a bow which He stretches and at a certain point says, "I can't stand any more," but God does not heed, He goes on stretching because He is aiming at His mark, not ours, and the patience of the saints is that they "hang in" until God lets the arrow fly.[24]

All of these saints saw the big picture and thought little of the immediate consequences.

Food for Thought

Examples of patience include waiting on the Lord and praising God in the midst of suffering. What examples, in addition to that of Paul and Silas, can you give—from the Bible or in your own life—that illustrate the value of patience?

For Further Study

- Read Psalm 40 to see the fruit of David's patience.
- In Romans 12:9–21, Paul shows step-by-step how to walk in love. And part of that walk requires us to be "patient in affliction" (v. 12).
- Abraham endured patiently and received God's promise (Genesis 21–22; Hebrews 6:15).
- At the end of Paul's second letter to Timothy (2 Timothy 4:6–8), he cites that patience has carried him through every trial and temptation.

Day 21

SET
APART

Therefore, since Christ suffered in his body, arm yourselves also with the same attitude, because he who has suffered in his body is done with sin. As a result, he does not live the rest of his earthly life for evil human desires, but rather for the will of God. For you have spent enough time in the past doing what pagans choose to do—living in debauchery, lust, drunkenness, orgies, carousing and detestable idolatry. They think it strange that you do not plunge with them into the same flood of dissipation, and they heap abuse on you. But they will have to give account to him who is ready to judge the living and the dead. For this is the reason the gospel was preached even to those who are now dead, so that they might be judged according to men in regard to the body, but live according to God in regard to the spirit.

The end of all things is near. Therefore be clear minded and self-controlled so that you can pray. Above all, love each other deeply, because love covers over a multitude of sins.

(1 PETER 4:1–8)

There are many ways that God sets apart His people. Mostly, being "set apart" means that we, like Jesus, are *in* the world but not *of* it. And throughout this devotional we are learning that we are also "set apart" for persecution.

Sometimes, however, as we will see in the following example provided by Open Doors Minister-at-Large Paul Estabrooks in *Secrets to Spiritual Success*, "set apart" means nothing less than a miracle.

Oswaldo Magdangal is a Filipino Christian who worked in Riyadh, Saudi Arabia, and pastored a secret house church. There has not been an official church of any kind in Saudi Arabia for over 1,400 years.

In late 1992, Oswaldo was arrested with a co-worker after a raid on their meeting place by the *muttawa*, the Saudi religious police. For three and a half hours he was physically and mentally tortured.

They slapped, boxed, and kicked him on the face. Then, using a long stick, they lashed his back and the palms of his hands. Then the soles of his feet. He could not stand without wincing, and he describes his bruised body as looking like an eggplant.

Upon returning to his cell, Oswaldo prayed for five hours, thanking God for allowing him to participate in the sufferings of Jesus. [In his book *Arrested in the Kingdom* (Open Doors U.K., 1993), Oswaldo recounts the moment.]

"Suddenly there was light. The cell was filled with the Lord's Shekinah glory. His presence was there. He knelt and started to touch my face. He told me, 'My son, I have seen all of it, that's why I'm here. I am assuring you that I will never leave you or forsake you.' "

Oswaldo awoke two hours later feeling like a new man. He was amazed when he saw his body had been restored to perfect wholeness. No bruises, no cuts, or bloodstains.[25]

A Few Observations

Throughout the first epistle of Peter, the apostle describes a people set apart for the Lord: "chosen according to the foreknowledge of God the Father" (1:2); "holy, because I am holy" (1:16); "born again, not of perishable seed, but of imperishable, through the living and enduring word of God" (1:23); and "a holy priesthood, offering spiritual sacrifices acceptable to God through Jesus Christ" (2:5).

Furthermore, we are those who are forbidden to "repay evil with evil or insult with insult, but with blessing, because to this you were called so that you may inherit a blessing" (3:9).

Trials, Peter explains, "come so that your faith—of greater worth than gold, which perishes even though refined by fire—may be proved genuine and may result in praise, glory and honor when Jesus Christ is revealed" (1:7).

Persecution for our devotion to, affection for, knowledge of, and resemblance to Christ is one way in which Christians are set apart. It is inseparable from holiness, because Christ is holy but was also "despised and rejected by men, a man of sorrows, and familiar with suffering" (Isaiah 53:3).

Food for Thought

Being set apart, in the context of 1 Peter, is not simply being isolated, shunned, or cut off. Our sins and even our personality are ungodly reasons

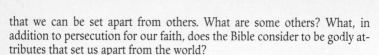

that we can be set apart from others. What are some others? What, in addition to persecution for our faith, does the Bible consider to be godly attributes that set us apart from the world?

For Further Study

- 1 Peter 2:9 declares that Christians "are a chosen people, a royal priesthood, a holy nation, a people belonging to God, that you may declare the praises of him who called you out of darkness into his wonderful light." We are called out. Separated. Set apart.
- Like Paul, we are set apart for the Gospel (Romans 1:1).
- Psalm 139:13–16 says we, like Paul (Galatians 1:15), were set apart from birth and called to serve God.
- We, like Christ (Hebrews 7:26), were set apart from sinners by His precious blood.
- And we are called to sanctify or set apart Christ as Lord in our hearts (1 Peter 3:15).

Day 22

FALSE
TEACHERS

But there were also false prophets among the people, just as there will be false teachers among you. They will secretly introduce destructive heresies, even denying the sovereign Lord who bought them—bringing swift destruction on themselves. Many will follow their shameful ways and will bring the way of truth into disrepute. In their greed these teachers will exploit you with stories they have made up. Their condemnation has long been hanging over them, and their destruction has not been sleeping.

(2 PETER 2:1–3)

Heresy is a major problem in China's house church movement. Leaders cite three main sources.

The first is when an individual's experience of God becomes elevated to a doctrine that everyone is required to accept. In southern Henan, for example, one house church movement requires everyone to receive a spirit-visitation from "the old self." Apparently, this is because the leader of this group came to faith when he had a vision of a ghost that he interpreted to be his dark self. This dark self warned him he was going to take him over. In terror, the man reached for the greater power of Jesus to defeat his dark self.

As a testimony, it is impressive. As a doctrine, it is nonsense.

Legalism is the second main source of heresy. Here, a biblical truth is pushed to an extreme and becomes an enslaving, rather than liberating, truth. One example is in varying interpretations of the doctrine of predestination.

Some groups say material blessing is God's sign that you are saved. Others say that, once you are saved, you are always saved and can live any way you please, because God is obligated to take to heaven those He has chosen. These doctrinal perversions clearly obscure the grace of God.

The third main source of heresy is folk religion, which carries over into the practice of the newfound Christian faith and can create distortions.

One participant testified of a visit to Heilongjiang Province where he noticed the church leaders making decisions using oracular blocks (two kidney-shaped wooden blocks, flat on one side and curved on the other, used as divination tools in traditional Chinese religions). A priest asks a yes or no question of the deity and throws the blocks up in the air. If one lands with the flat side up and the other with the curved side up, the god has said yes. Both flat sides down means no, and both curved sides down means, "try again."

Church leaders based this on a passage in Acts 1 that says the disciples chose to replace Judas by "casting lots" to determine which of two candidates should serve. With this scriptural encouragement, leaders would "cast the blocs" at the Lord's Supper to determine who should be a deacon, elder, or evangelist. Needless to say, the method resulted in some very unsuitable people being placed in leadership positions.

Heresies are best combated by intensive Scripture training.

According to one fifty-three-year-old co-worker from Wenzhou, "We used to think heresies would disappear with Bibles arriving. But in our area, we have plenty of Bibles and still heresy persists. We see the need not only to bring the Scriptures but also to teach the right interpretation of the Scriptures."[26]

A Few Observations

Paul told the saints at Corinth, "I resolved to know nothing while I was with you except Jesus Christ and him crucified" (1 Corinthians 2:2). And he warns all believers in Romans 14:1, to "accept him whose faith is weak, without passing judgment on disputable matters."

The church must return to the ministry of John the Baptist, that is, pointing everyone to Jesus. Not to churches, doctrines, or denominations.

Heresy and false teaching are two of Satan's most vicious and deadly weapons against the persecuted church. They divide and destroy the church, and thus are far more devastating than imprisonment and martyrdom, which have always caused the church to grow.

Western believers, too, must wade cautiously through the abundance of teaching that is engulfing the church, avoiding disputable matters and trusting those who point to Jesus.

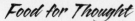

Food for Thought

Doctrine divides. But Jesus says in John 12:32, "But I, when I am lifted up from the earth, will draw all men to myself." Where believers may be divided on doctrine, we must be united in Christ. What are some of the doctrines that divide Christians today and the consequences of those divisions? If you have been involved in increasing divisions among believers, take the opportunity right now to repent and ask God to forgive you. Pray regularly for unity in the church worldwide.

For Further Study

- Read Jesus' teaching on division in Luke 11:17.
- In 1 Corinthians 1:10, Paul appeals for unity in the church.
- Division is a sign of an immature church, Paul says in 1 Corinthians 3:3.
- There should be no divisions in the body of Christ, says 1 Corinthians 12:25.
- Romans 16:17 says believers are to avoid those who cause divisions.
- Proverbs 6:16–19 lists six things the Lord hates. The sixth is "a man who stirs up dissension among brothers."

Suggested Activity

Bibles are in extremely short supply in countries like China and Sudan, making patience a survival virtue. In Vietnam, some believers have to memorize Psalm 119 before church leaders will put them on a waiting list to receive a Bible. Try to memorize Psalm 119 with your family or a group of friends by dividing the chapters into sections.

Day 23

ANTICHRIST

Dear friends, do not believe every spirit, but test the spirits to see whether they are from God, because many false prophets have gone out into the world. This is how you can recognize the Spirit of God: Every spirit that acknowledges that Jesus Christ has come in the flesh is from God, but every spirit that does not acknowledge Jesus is not from God. This is the spirit of the antichrist, which you have heard is coming and even now is already in the world.

(1 JOHN 4:1–3)

Following are excerpts from the diary of a forty-year-old itinerant evangelist traveling around China's Zhejiang province:

> Arrived in a small town, but a local Daoist priest heard of my coming, and came to the house chanting his scriptures and banging a gong. He treated me like an evil spirit. I came out to pray for him face to face, but he began to curse me. He ran off to fetch the Public Security Bureau (secret police), so reluctantly I quit the town, but not before arranging to meet the members of the house church later. We had a wonderful night of prayer in the fields outside the town. Prayed from nine at night till the dawn together. . . .
>
> Very special. God came close. It was as if the stars sat on our shoulders. We embraced. I shared from the Scriptures for three hours strengthening them. . . .
>
> We tend to legalism in China. Must be our Confucian heritage. Someone in our leadership council wanted to insist that we each brand ourselves with the sign of the Cross. Another wanted us to produce a statement requiring everyone to speak Scripture aloud, declaring it to be more effective than inward reading. At every Council meeting we fight this

same battle against legalism . . . just like Paul had to confront the Juda-
izers time and time again. . . .

Oh dear. Cult problems. One of our co-workers in northern Jiangsu
has been teaching his groups to chant his name alongside Christ's, and
he has written choruses all must sing or face excommunication. We received reports that every issue in the church is about loyalty. Everyone is
assessed purely on the question—are you loyal to me or not? I give a talk
that honesty is more important than loyalty, and we will send the tape.
Chances are he will leave our movement rather than submit. It seems the
only way that we can control heresy is to lay down the law. . . .

I leave again on another two-month swing through five provinces. I
will hear of great healings, and of great persecution. God is glorified in
the darkness and the light. That's why He's the Great God, the only One
whose Gospel is for everyone in China. God grant me a long life to share
His Good News with as many as I can.[27]

A Few Observations

In the past decade, the world has seen a veritable epidemic of cults. At the
same time, Islam, which loudly—and often violently—denies that God has a
Son, has become the fastest-growing religion on earth.

Cults are most dangerous to the weak and isolated. They pick off the
stragglers, just as wild dogs devour the young and infirm zebra or gazelles in
the herds.

Islam, however, consumes entire nations. And beneath the shadow of the
star and crescent, persecution of Christians is the most intense.

Food for Thought

It is vital to remember that Muslims are not the enemies of Christians.
Brother Andrew likes to illustrate this by turning the word Islam into the
acronym ISLAM—"I Sincerely Love All Muslims." As we hear God's wake-
up call to the church to be aware of and minister to our persecuted brothers
and sisters, we must be oh-so-cautious that we do not allow Satan to paint
the lost—any lost—with the brush of anger, bitterness, or violence. Always,
in every circumstance, our attitude must be one of love, the posture of Christ.

For Further Study

- 1 Corinthians 12:10 lists "to distinguish between spirits" as one of the
  gifts of the Spirit, along with words of wisdom and knowledge, gifts of
  healing, and the working of miracles.

- Luke 9:52–55 tells of Jesus being rejected in Samaria, and when the Sons of Thunder, James and John, saw this, they asked Him if they should call down fire from heaven to consume the Samaritans. And Jesus turned and rebuked them, saying, "You do not know what kind of spirit you are of" (v. 55 NASB).
- Peter did not recognize the spirit that prompted him to tempt Jesus away from His mission. But Jesus recognized it, saying, "Get behind me, Satan! You are a stumbling block to me; you do not have in mind the things of God, but the things of men" (Matthew 16:22–23).
- 2 Timothy 1:7 speaks of a spirit of fear, of power, and of love.
- 1 Samuel 16:14 speaks of an evil spirit that tormented Saul.
- And Acts 16:16–18 tells of a devilish spirit of fortune-telling cast out by Paul.
- Mark 1:23 tells of an unclean spirit in the synagogue at Capernaum; Mark 5:1–13 of an entire legion of spirits in a man in the Gadarenes; and Mark 9:14–29 of a spirit that would come out only by prayer and fasting.

Day 24

BEWARE!

Many deceivers, who do not acknowledge Jesus Christ as coming in the flesh, have gone out into the world. Any such person is the deceiver and the antichrist. Watch out that you do not lose what you have worked for, but that you may be rewarded fully. Anyone who runs ahead and does not continue in the teaching of Christ does not have God; whoever continues in the teaching has both the Father and the Son. If anyone comes to you and does not bring this teaching, do not take him into your house or welcome him. Anyone who welcomes him shares in his wicked work.

(2 JOHN 7–11)

A house church member in China shared the following story with Alex Buchan of Open Doors.

> We had followed Christ for five years before we met Brother Chen Zhun. There were twenty believers in our village in rural Hubei province. Our church began as a result of listening to Christian radio, and when my mother was healed of appendicitis, two whole families converted to the way of Jesus.
>
> When Brother Chen arrived one spring, some said he was "sent straight from God to our company." He said so too. Looking back over a year later, I think he was Satan's man. But who knows, I may be harsh in my judgment.
>
> I remember that night so clearly. We were all gathered in my father's house. The gas lamp flickered strange shapes against the whitewashed walls, on which we had stenciled "JESUS IS THE WAY, THE TRUTH, AND THE LIFE."
>
> Chen was an impressive looking young man of maybe thirty. He said

he had known Wang Ming Dao, but we didn't know who he was. We were just excited that someone from the great city of Shanghai had come to see us—we who were never visited by anyone.

He spoke into the expectant silence with a loud booming voice. His large eyes held our attention closely, and his whole body shook with the vigor of the points he was making.

To tell you the truth, I don't remember what he said that first night. We were just so impressed with the way he talked. He quoted lots of Scripture, wove it into a thrilling story, told us we were missing out on so many blessings, and that he was here to lead us to Jesus. He left us all looking at each other with a mixture of excitement and unease. We were missing the way, but how?

Brother Chen stayed on to tell us how.

From that moment on, our meetings changed. He was the leader. Until then, we had read from a Bible, discussed the passage, and written off our questions to a Bible teacher in Beijing.

But we found the Bible very difficult, and none of us knew what it meant. Most of us could not read the hard and strange words, and there were so many of them. We enjoyed prayer, however, and our meetings could go long into the night, often with shouts of joy or times of reverent silence. We felt God close.

But Chen began to teach us something more. "To really know Jesus," he said, "we all have to go through three gates."

He explained that the first was the gate of tears. He claimed that Jesus said, "Blessed are they that weep." So he taught us to cry. It was wonderful at first. We just rolled around weeping, groaning, and wailing. After a few months, he said we were ready to enter the second gate.

But two of our company said they could not weep as uncontrollably as the rest. For the first time we saw Brother Chen angry.

"Do not resist the will of God," he boomed at them. "Do not turn yourself over to Satan."

He forbade them to come to the meetings any more, until they could cry as uncontrollably as the rest of us. But they never came back and began to spread a bad report about us in the rest of the village.

Next, we learned about the gate of childlike faith. "Jesus said we have to come unto him like little children," he told us. "Children are trusting, giving, and simple-minded. They obey their parents if they know what's good for them."

Brother Chen didn't say so in as many words, but a few months later we were all sure that he saw himself as the parent and us as the children.

Why did we not see this coming?

Well, he seemed to speak the words of God. He knew the Bible. He had a verse for everything, and we could not check for ourselves because few of us could read really well.

Six months later, even though we were smaller in number, we felt inspired by him, like it was a treat to sit at his feet and hear him talk of Jesus.

The third gate was what he called the "gate of gold," or "the golden gate." I know he had Scriptures for this one too, but I can't remember them. I think it was something about heaven being a city of gold, and that to enter that city we would have to demonstrate that we had given Jesus our gold in our lifetime.

"Jesus needs our gold to build our mansion in heaven," I remember Brother Chen saying, "and the more gold we give him now, the bigger your mansion will be."

Well, we were poor. And because we were poor, the idea of having a golden mansion in the afterlife was very tempting to us. We handed over all we owned: family heirlooms, money, some expensive textiles from a distant ancestor. One of our group even gave his motorcycle, which he had saved for years to buy.

Looking back, we should have known what was happening. But we trusted him, and saw no reason to doubt his teaching. He was moral and humble, a gracious houseguest who helped in the fields as needed. We never found out much about him. He never really shared himself with us, and that should have made us suspicious.

After all the "gold" had been collected, Brother Chen said he had to go and "open the gate for us." He left on the motorcycle that had been donated. He took most of our savings. And he hasn't been back.

Now the fellowship is ruined. Some of our group believe he is coming back and was indeed sent by God to help us know Jesus better. Others of us, like myself, believe he was a deceiver and that his teaching was carefully designed to part us from our "gold" from the beginning.

It has split my family. My father thinks Chen was a good man. The rest of the family think differently, but we dare not disagree with my father openly.

We still can't read the Bible very well. We really don't know that much about Jesus, to be honest. We know He has saved us and healed a family member. But we know little else.[28]

A Few Observations

The word translated *antichrist* appears only four times in Scripture (five times in the King James Version)—all in John's first two letters. The Greek word means literally *instead of the Messiah*. The term is used to refer to a spirit rather than an actual person, such as the Beast of Revelation. And that spirit is present in anyone who denies or dilutes the deity of Jesus Christ.

For every Christian, especially believers suffering persecution, faith must be founded upon an ongoing, intimate, personal relationship with the living Christ. If our foundation is built upon a watery literary character, we will fall under temptation and flee before persecution. And anyone who accepts Jesus as no more than a good man or a prophet—even the best man who ever lived—and denies that He is God incarnate, has the spirit of antichrist and preaches someone other than the Messiah.

Lest any think they cannot fall, recall Jesus' warning in Matthew 24:11 that "many false prophets will appear and deceive many people," and again in verses 23–24, "At that time if anyone says to you, 'Look, here is the Christ!' or 'There he is!' do not believe it. For false Christs and false prophets will appear and perform great signs and miracles to deceive even the elect—if that were possible."

Pray for discernment for the persecuted church, that they will recognize the spirit of antichrist wherever and however it appears and that they will not be led away by manifestations and false doctrines.

Food for Thought

Do you think a spirit of antichrist is at work in your country? What is it doing? What are some subtle things today that are leading believers away from Jesus? How can believers learn to recognize and expose the spirit of antichrist?

For Further Study

- The antichrist spirit is behind many of the things that are prophesied to happen in the last days. Read Isaiah 2.
- Also read Daniel 12.
- Micah 4 also tells of the signs of the times.
- 2 Timothy 3:1–9 paints a vivid picture of the fruit of the antichrist spirit, as does 2 Peter 3.
- Read Matthew 24 and Mark 13.

Suggested Activity

Research what the Koran says about Jesus, and find the passages in Scripture that tell the truth about Him. Visit a mosque, and talk with the imam

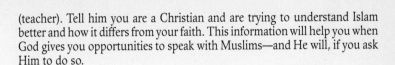

(teacher). Tell him you are a Christian and are trying to understand Islam better and how it differs from your faith. This information will help you when God gives you opportunities to speak with Muslims—and He will, if you ask Him to do so.

Day 25

GODLESS LEADERS

I wrote to the church, but Diotrephes, who loves to be first, will have nothing to do with us. So if I come, I will call attention to what he is doing, gossiping maliciously about us. Not satisfied with that, he refuses to welcome the brothers. He also stops those who want to do so and puts them out of the church.

(3 JOHN 9–10)

House church leaders in China representing over ten million members met for a conference in the summer of 1998 to discuss the main problems facing their churches.

At the top of the list was gossip. Leader after leader told stories of how their ministries had been compromised by this subtle sin. One house church leader in Henan shared this experience:

I went into an area to lead Bible studies for co-workers and found they would not let me into the house where we were holding the seminar. I asked them through the closed door what the problem was, but they wouldn't tell me. They just told me to go away.

It was winter, and I prepared to go a little way outside the town to sleep rough, knowing I must start a fire to sleep beside or I would freeze to death. I wondered what on earth could have made those brothers and sisters turn me away into such a cold night without a word of explanation.

But a brother took pity on me and brought me secretly to his home. I pried the truth out of him eventually. The leaders in the area had received an anonymous letter denouncing me as a "lover of many women."

Try as I might, I could not get them to listen to me and let me see the letter.

Later, in another part of the country, I learned the letter had been sent

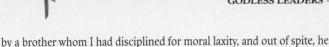

by a brother whom I had disciplined for moral laxity, and out of spite, he sent it to the place where I was going.

I went to him and he was repentant. He sent another letter, but because the first one was unsigned, they had no way to believe him. Both of us offered to go there, but we were not welcomed at all. The testimony of the church was ruined. I still have to explain myself wherever I go, and it is just a victory for the devil.

I took the offending brother out to the countryside and told him to pluck a chicken. We walked along while he did; the wind blew the feathers far over the fields.

"What now?" he asked, when he was finished.

"Pick up every feather, and put it back on the chicken," I told him.

"That's impossible," he complained.

"You are right. It is impossible, just as the damage your words have done cannot be repaired."

Leaders pledged to be more loving and to hold more face-to-face meetings with each other to minimize what they called "the demon of gossip."

Said one leader, "Xu Yongze is in jail today because of our gossip against his group."[29]

A Few Observations

The persecution that perhaps causes the deepest wounds is that caused by other believers, especially those in leadership. Their weapons are gossip and slander. They are manipulators and abusers of authority. They are false shepherds who are more interested in building their own kingdoms than the kingdom of God and are busy drawing people to themselves rather than to Christ. Instead of feeding the sheep, they fleece them. Here, too, the spirit of antichrist is at work.

And not only in false shepherds but also in denominations that puff themselves up, separating believers, slandering other denominations, and rejecting those who believe, pray, or worship differently. They believe the truth to be resident only in them.

This type of persecution is not limited to Asia, Africa, and the Middle East. It takes its toll throughout the West as well.

Food for Thought

If you or someone you know is a victim of false shepherds or denominational divisions, use this time for healing, prayer, and, if necessary, repentance. Ask the Holy Spirit to enable you to forgive anyone who has wounded you. And ask Him to show you whether you have caused division among brethren or abused the authority He has given you as a husband, wife, parent, or leader. If so, confess it as sin, receive God's forgiveness, and be reconciled. Finally, pray for your brethren in the persecuted church who have been wounded.

For Further Study

- False shepherds have preyed on God's people from the beginning. The Lord chastises them in Isaiah 56.
- Jeremiah 23 and 50 says Israel's false shepherds have scattered the flock and led the sheep astray.
- Ezekiel 34 rebukes false shepherds for using and abusing the sheep in their care for their own personal gain.
- John 10:12 warns about what we can expect from hirelings.

Day 26

BUILD YOURSELVES UP!

But, dear friends, remember what the apostles of our Lord Jesus Christ foretold. They said to you, "In the last times there will be scoffers who will follow their own ungodly desires." These are the men who divide you, who follow mere natural instincts and do not have the Spirit. But you, dear friends, build yourselves up in your most holy faith and pray in the Holy Spirit. Keep yourselves in God's love as you wait for the mercy of our Lord Jesus Christ to bring you to eternal life.

(JUDE 17–21)

We are all part of the same fellowship of believers, which the Bible calls the body of Christ. We need one another. And for decades, Open Doors has supported and encouraged believers in persecuted lands. Oftentimes, though, it takes just one person to make an impact, even save lives.

During the difficult times in Romania, a young believer was called in to the secret police for interrogation. He had dreaded this moment. Fear gripped him throughout, and he struggled with the police department's offer of good prospects and security if he would inform on his fellow-believers.

He did not accept the offer, but his inability to reject it unquestioningly brought personal agony. He could not sleep that night, trembling from fear and guilt.

The next morning, led by the Spirit of God, an older Christian came to visit the family. He was unaware of the young man's dilemma, but being a former prisoner for the faith himself, he was able to discern the problem and give counsel to the young man from Scripture.

He built up the young man in fellowship, training him for the next interrogation ordeal, which came the next afternoon.

The young man was still upset about his answers the second time; and again the older believer came to encourage him.

Three days passed in this fashion.

Eventually the young man was able to reject the police offer completely. He was released.

Discernment, counsel, prayer, and patient care had brought him through and trained him in righteousness.[30]

A Few Observations

Persecution is inevitable. And the safest place to receive it is wrapped in the arms of Jesus.

Since Christians cannot avoid persecution, we must build ourselves up to withstand it, to endure, to persevere in order to win the prize and reach the goal God has set before us.

This is the mission of Open Doors given to Brother Andrew through Revelation 3:2 in 1954: "Be watchful, and strengthen the things which remain, that are ready to die."

By prayer, visitations, bringing in Bibles, and training new leaders, we prepare the church for persecution and strengthen it in the midst of suffering. And the heart and focus of everything is Jesus. It is all aimed at developing and deepening the believer's intimate relationship with Him.

Whether Jesus fans the flames away from us as He did alongside the Hebrew children in the Babylonian furnace, or provides a beatific vision as He did when Stephen was being stoned to death, or makes the most intense pain tolerable as with Bishops Ridley and Latimer, He is our shelter. He is our strong tower who will never leave us or forsake us.

Food for Thought

Spend this time in worship. If you are alone and play an instrument, play and sing to the Lord. If you are in a group, turn on a worship cassette. You can also use this time to write a love letter or poem to Jesus, expressing the depth of your affection for Him.

For Further Study

- Paul has an edifying word for the church in Acts 20:32.
- The strong are called to build up the weak (Romans 15:1–6).
- The spiritual gifts are for the building up of the church (1 Corinthians 14:1–25).
- We are commanded to encourage one another (1 Thessalonians 5:11).

Day 27

PROMISES FOR ENDURANCE

"He who has an ear, let him hear what the Spirit says to the churches. To him who overcomes, I will give the right to eat from the tree of life, which is in the paradise of God. . . .

He who has an ear, let him hear what the Spirit says to the churches. He who overcomes will not be hurt at all by the second death. . . .

He who has an ear, let him hear what the Spirit says to the churches. To him who overcomes, I will give some of the hidden manna. I will also give him a white stone with a new name written on it, known only to him who receives it. . . .

To him who overcomes and does my will to the end, I will give authority over the nations—'He will rule them with an iron scepter; he will dash them to pieces like pottery'—just as I have received authority from my Father. . . .

He who overcomes will, like them, be dressed in white. I will never blot out his name from the book of life, but will acknowledge his name before my Father and his angels. . . .

Him who overcomes I will make a pillar in the temple of my God. Never again will he leave it. I will write on him the name of my God and the name of the city of my God, the new Jerusalem, which is coming down out of heaven from my God; and I will also write on him my new name. . . .

To him who overcomes, I will give the right to sit with me on my throne, just as I overcame and sat down with my Father on his throne."

(REVELATION 2:7, 11, 17, 26–27; 3:5, 12, 21)

Pastor Ung Sophal established eight house churches in Phnom Penh, Cambodia, and the surrounding provinces. Here, Open Doors Minister-at-Large Paul Estabrooks shares Pastor Sophal's story.

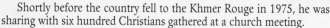

Shortly before the country fell to the Khmer Rouge in 1975, he was sharing with six hundred Christians gathered at a church meeting.

Aware of the danger ahead, they agreed to write their names on the back wall of the church building if they made it back to Phnom Penh. Only three names were ever to appear on the wall—that of Ung and two others who narrowly escaped death.

He and his wife lost their third and youngest child during the genocide. After many close calls, Ung was separated from his wife and children and sent to work in the fields. During these very difficult times, he still was able to lead sixty-five people to Jesus and even water baptize them. God miraculously spared his life on numerous occasions.

When the Vietnamese invaded Kampuchea (formerly Cambodia) in 1979, Ung Sophal was able to return to Phnom Penh. It was now a ghost town. With a handful of other Christians, he started a house church, which grew from five members to six hundred in eight months.

That Christmas, he invited some Christians—including some Westerners who worked for aid organizations—to his home for fellowship.

As a result, two weeks later he was arrested for this "illegal" activity and accused of holding a political meeting with CIA participation.

He was interrogated for days and beaten severely. When the interrogation proved profitless, he was left in prison for five months chained hand and foot. He lost seventy-five pounds and was very sick, but he heard the Lord instruct him to fast and be silent for three days.

The authorities became alarmed at the end of his fast and took him to the hospital thinking he was dying. There, he constantly heard the sounds of other people being tortured with electricity and being beaten and kicked.

"Even without the beatings it was very hard," [he told a *Los Angeles Times* reporter]. "I had a taste of Hell, but God protected me."

Ung Sophal was successfully treated by a Cuban doctor who was also a Christian. And one night, when the electricity went out because of a tropical storm, the doctor helped Ung escape.

Later, he escaped with his wife and children to Thailand and spent ten years ministering to other Cambodian exiles—the last five years as a widower. Here is how [Andrew Wark's Asian report for Open Doors] concludes:

"In 1990, as restrictions against Christianity began to be eased in Cambodia, Ung made his first visit back to his homeland to encourage and teach the church. Word of his return spread quickly and three hundred people came to see him.

"Cambodia's Prime Minister also requested to see Ung. During a forty-minute meeting, the pastor shared his vision for rebuilding the ravaged nation, including his plans to establish orphanages, educational facilities, and hospitals.

"Ung is eager for the task ahead.

" 'I want to build my people,' he said. 'God has a great work yet to do in Cambodia.' "[31]

A Few Observations

Jesus "was willing to die a shameful death on the cross because of the joy he knew would be his afterwards" (Hebrews 12:2 TLB). So it is with the believer.

"The joy of the Lord is your strength," said Nehemiah (8:10).

Psalm 51:12 speaks of "the joy of your salvation." What is that joy? It's the joy of freedom from the bondage of sin. It's our escape from the flames. It's the peace that comes with being reconciled to God. It's the joy set before us—being the servant, friend, brother, sister, and bride of Christ.

It's eating the fruit of the Tree of Life, escaping the Second Death, having a white stone with our new name on it, ruling nations, possessing the Morning Star (Jesus), being clothed in purity and righteousness with one's name inscribed in the Book of Life, being secure and possessed by God, living in God's city, and sitting with Him on His throne.

The joy set before us is nothing less than eternal life. "Now this is eternal life: that they may know you, the only true God, and Jesus Christ, whom you have sent" (John 17:3).

Food for Thought

A ballplayer can endure rigorous exercise and workouts, verbal abuse from the coach—anything, when he is focused entirely on the reward of playing ball. What sacrifices have you willingly, even gladly, made for something you wanted very badly? What sacrifices are necessary to enter God's kingdom? What place do sacrifice and suffering play in the Christian life after being "saved"?

For Further Study

- "Where there is no vision, the people perish" (Proverbs 29:18 KJV).
- The rewards for suffering persecution are not to be found on earth (Matthew 5:11–12).

- Jesus will reward each person according to what he has done (Matthew 16:27).
- Colossians 3:23–24 offers another promise of reward.
- Moses was an excellent example of one who endured much, looking ahead to his reward (Hebrews 11:6).
- And the final and greatest promise is to be found in Revelation 22:12. For our best reward is Jesus himself.

Suggested Activity

Most of us have never experienced persecution like our brothers and sisters in hostile countries. To gain a little more understanding, conduct a Bible study with friends in a dark, isolated area. No one can have a Bible. There can be no musical instruments, no overheads, no hymnals, no lights. You must arrive at intervals in ones and twos from different directions. If you sing or speak, it must be in whispers, lest you are caught and punished. Whoever is designated as the leader or pastor can share only from memorized passages and must preach without notes.

Many of these meetings last for hours, because the brethren cannot get enough of it. When you leave, do so the way you came—quietly, at intervals, and in ones and twos. (When organizing this, you might arrange for someone to take the role of the secret police and see what the group of Christians does when they hear "someone" approaching in the distance.)

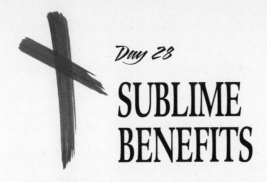

Day 28

SUBLIME BENEFITS

Stephen, full of the Holy Spirit, looked up to heaven and saw the glory of God, and Jesus standing at the right hand of God. "Look," he said, "I see heaven open and the Son of Man standing at the right hand of God"

(ACTS 7:55).

Zinaida Vilchinskaya was a grandmother at the time she was arrested while carrying Christian literature in the former Soviet Union. She shares the following:

> When the police first took me to the police station, I was put in a very cold cell with bare iron bunks. The guards took my scarf and my coat, and I lay on the bunk in just a dress. I was shivering, and I started to pray. When my cellmate saw me pray, she, too, got on her knees and said, "Oh, I can't stand it. I'm freezing too." She started to cry softly.
>
> "Lord," I prayed, "if you want me to be frozen here, may your will be done; just enable me to endure this with love, submission, and meekness. But you can help me. You can even take me out of here if that's your will."
>
> I lay back down and felt such warmth. I told the other woman, "Here, let me put my arm around you, and you'll get warmer." We warmed up together. Later when they transferred us to different cells, she told everyone in hers, "God warmed up Aunt Zhenya [as they called me] in our cell, and she warmed me up."[32]

A Few Observations

James, the son of Zebedee, was beheaded—the first of the Twelve to be martyred. Matthew, tradition holds, was also beheaded. Peter, Andrew, Jude, and Bartholomew were crucified. Thomas was run through with spears and thrown into an oven.

In some accounts of God's precious martyrs, great suffering was evident. In others, as with Stephen, the brother or sister appears to experience little or no pain.

For us, there are no guarantees but one: with or without pain, we will not die alone. And this is our sublime benefit, our ace in the hole.

"As I was with Moses," God promised Joshua, "so I will be with you; I will never leave you nor forsake you" (Joshua 1:5). His promise is for us as well.

"And surely I am with you always," Jesus said, "to the very end of the age" (Matthew 28:20).

With our eyes fixed steadfastly upon Jesus, all else pales and fades out of focus. The apostles rejoiced in their suffering, not because they were made of sterner stuff than we are, but because the pain and shame were of such little account, compared to the privilege of sharing *anything* with Jesus—including His suffering.

Food for Thought

It would be wonderful if there was an exercise or experiment that would allow us to test God's faithfulness in the midst of suffering. Something on a very small scale, so if it didn't work, it wouldn't hurt too much or do permanent damage. Then again, perhaps it would not be so wonderful after all. If indeed the Christian lives by faith, as Paul says in 2 Corinthians 5:7, we must also suffer and die by that same faith. Like the verse in a popular song says, "When you can't see His hands, trust His heart." We will not know experientially that He will be there until we get there. But our faith should assure us that He will.

For Further Study

- The Lord is near to all who call on Him (Psalm 145:18).
- The key to closeness to God lies in our own hands (James 4:8).
- Wherever we go or whatever happens to us in this life, we can depend on a sense of divine rest in the midst of turmoil (Exodus 33:14).
- Isaiah 43:2 seems to guarantee safety from drowning or burning. Yet, we have seen many precious saints burned or drowned for their faith. Where then is the comfort in this promise? It is in the assurance of His presence and that neither water nor flames can destroy His love for us or our immortal soul.

Day 29

PERSECUTION PROPHESIED

You understand, O Lord; remember me and care for me. Avenge me on my persecutors. You are long-suffering—do not take me away; think of how I suffer reproach for your sake.

(JEREMIAH 15:15)

A community of Russian Christians in Chuguyevka, Siberia, shared how their many difficulties did not deter evangelistic outreach but rather encouraged it:

> Right at the start, God had warned them that they would encounter difficult times, and the prophecy had made them strong and courageous. They knew that God's plan ensured them victory in the end.
>
> Nobody gave any thought to giving in to proposals of people such as Chupin [KGB officer]. Worship services continued, just as their evangelism and widespread Bible teaching did. Using two wrecked cars that had been restored and four motorcycles, a number of evangelistic teams spread out each week. . . .
>
> The Chuguyevka evangelists were eminently practical. If they met a Christian who had lived alone for years and complained about loneliness, they would ask, "Does anyone at work know you are a Christian?"
>
> Often the person would say no, and then they would offer this advice: "OK, start by telling your colleagues at work that God loves them." More often than not a fellow worker would also be present on their next visit.[33]

A Few Observations

Long before the advent of Christianity, God warned that those who loved Him would be persecuted by Satan, who hates Him and everything that is His.

"O Lord my God," David cried, "I take refuge in you; save and deliver me from all who pursue me, or they will tear me like a lion and rip me to pieces with no one to rescue me" (Psalm 7:1).

Sounds remarkably like the cry of Ignatius in A.D. 110, moments before he walked into the arena of Emperor Trajan to face the hungry lions: "I am the wheat of Christ: I am going to be ground with the teeth of wild beasts that I may be found pure bread."

And in Psalm 119:86, David spoke prophetically of the future church when he declared, "All your commands are trustworthy; help me, for men persecute me without cause."

Persecution of God's people was prophesied centuries before Jesus came. We should not be surprised that it continues—and even increases—today.

Food for Thought

What goes through your mind when you hear about religious persecution, torture, and martyrdom? Does it all seem so far off that you feel you are unlikely to experience it? Does it grip you with fear? Does it fill you with compassion for your suffering brothers and sisters and drive you to your knees? Take your doubts and fears to the Lord in prayer. And while you are in your prayer closet, ask Him to fill the hearts of the persecuted church with His love, courage, and peace.

For Further Study

- Despite persecution, the grace is there for us to remain steadfast in our faith (Psalm 119:157).
- God's Word strengthens our heart against persecution (Psalm 119:161).
- David reveals the secret of surviving persecution and suffering in Psalm 143:9.

Day 30

MASTER JESUS

*"Remember the words I spoke to you: 'No servant is greater than his master.'
If they persecuted me, they will persecute you also"*

(JOHN 15:20).

We know from Jesus that persecution is inevitable. As His servants, we will face adversity and danger. Yet, like the apostle Paul and so many others, we are to forge ahead. "Forgetting what is behind and straining toward what is ahead, I press on toward the goal to win the prize for which God has called me heavenward in Christ Jesus" (Philippians 3:13–14).

Pastor Joseph Bondarenko exemplifies this God-driven spirit like few others. Here, Open Doors Minister-at-Large Paul Estabrooks introduces us to the Russian-speaking pastor of a church in Riga, Latvia.

Pastor Joseph Bondarenko sat on the sunny deck of the Russian river boat as it pulled out of Tyumen in Siberia and headed north up the river. The leaves on the trees were already changing color in a blaze of autumn beauty.

But this was no Love Boat. On board this old river scow were over one hundred and fifty other Christians joining this adventure—or what others later called a *cruise-ade*.

The passengers were there to assist in a one-month evangelism outreach in northern Siberian cities—places where the Gospel had never been preached before.

As Joseph soaked in the beauty of the sun and God's creation, he thought back on his early ministry years in the fifties and sixties. His aggressive evangelism in those days resulted in three prison sentences. Yet there in those filthy prison cells, God was still present, and his ministry continued. Joseph led so many to Christ in prison that they kicked him out each time.

He lived a total of nine years in a prison cell, isolated from his beloved wife, Mary.

Joseph smiled to himself as he recalled that eventful day in 1989 when the KGB agent who had him imprisoned came to talk.

The officer had been watching him for years and now expressed his desire to know Jesus, too.

Joseph's spirit leaped with joy as he thought back on the day that KGB agent and his family were baptized. Nothing is impossible with God.

He relived the many crusades in recent years when Open Doors provided as many as twenty thousand Russian Scriptures for new believers who responded to the call of God on their life.

And now with a group of musicians, preachers, and follow-up personnel, his vision for evangelism was continuing to be fulfilled. For the past month, he had preached at twenty cities along the main rivers of Siberia.

At the end of the month, Joseph's *cruise-ade* had seen over ten thousand people pray the sinner's prayer and commit their lives to the Lord! And even more exciting, Christian young people were left behind in sixteen communities to do follow-up training and establish a new church.

A few years ago, a ministry team visited Joseph's church in Riga, Latvia.

The most important room was in the back of the church. It was their "spiritual war room." On its walls were the missionary journey history of this local body and the missionary vision maps.

Joseph became animated and excited as he traced the color-coded missionary journeys for the past few summers that the young evangelists he was training had made into Siberia and onward toward the Far East.

But more exciting for him were the dotted lines that laid out next summer's trip plans. They reached right to the Pacific Ocean!

Like his Master, Joseph went through much suffering and deprivation in his life. But like his Master, nothing gave Joseph more joy than knowing the angels in heaven were rejoicing.[34]

A Few Observations

Being a slave or a serf had few benefits to commend it. But one of them was the assurance of protection, if only because slaves and serfs were considered property, and a lord or baron was fiercely protective of his property.

God, too, promises us His protection throughout Scripture.

For I am convinced that neither death nor life, neither angels nor demons, neither the present nor the future, nor any powers, neither height nor depth, nor anything else in all creation, will be able to separate us from the love of God that is in Christ Jesus our Lord. (Romans 8:38–39)

On the other hand, when one ruler attacked another, the fate of the vanquished ruler was the fate of his people. They were not spared when their lord or master was taken.

So it is with us. As they did to our Master, Jesus, they will do with us.

However, let us "rejoice and be glad, because great is your reward in heaven, for in the same way they persecuted the prophets who were before you" (Matthew 5:12).

And even now, we share in the eternal inheritance of His Son, ruling with Him forever!

Food for Thought

We have come to our final day, and what are our conclusions? We have encountered persecution, looked it full in the face, and discovered that it is far less terrible than we had been led to believe. We have learned that it is part and parcel of the normal Christian life. In fact, if we are indeed *in Christ*, persecution should be considered inevitable.

We have also learned that we can embrace persecution with joy and need not shun it out of fear. It *is* painful, yes. But compared to the sweet intimacy with Jesus . . . well, there is no comparison. Let us now ask the Holy Spirit to share with us His own compassion for the suffering church. May He give us a spirit of intercession on their behalf and the boldness to declare the love and mercy of our Lord without fear—until He returns.

"Even so, come, Lord Jesus."

Notes

Every effort was made to contact copyright holders for permission to use their material in this book. If there has been an oversight, please contact the publisher so that a correction can be made in future printings.

1. Paul Negrut, Romanian pastor. Audiocassette of message presented at Open Doors International headquarters, Holland, April 1990.
2. Paul Estabrooks, translated from a plaque at the Martyr's Memorial outside Seoul, South Korea.
3. Paul Estabrooks, *Secrets to Spiritual Success* (Tonbridge, U.K.: Sovereign World, 1996), 27–28.
4. Terry Brand, "God's Love Overcomes," *Open Doors Newsbrief* (July–August 1990), 3.
5. Estabrooks, *Secrets to Spiritual Success*, 132.
6. Dorothy Ai Chung, "How God Taught Me Brokenness," Christian Aid brochure (Charlottesville, Va.).
7. Wilson Chen, "I Learned the Hard Way, But I Learned," *Christianity Today* (March 19, 1982), 24.
8. Bill Harding IV, "Hearing the Songs of Praise in Ethiopia," *Decision* magazine (November 1991), 18.
9. John Foxe, *Foxe's Book of Martyrs*, SAGE Software [CD-ROM] Version 1.0. (Albany, Ore., 1996), 29.

10. David Y. P. Wang, "Eight Lessons We Can Learn From the Church in China," Asian Outreach International publication (Hong Kong), 5–7.

11. F. Kefa Sempangi with Barbara R. Thompson, *A Distant Grief* (Glendale, Calif.: Regal Books, 1979), 119–121. EDITOR'S NOTE: The context of the quoted material was adapted from *A Distant Grief*; the quotes are accurate.

12. Negrut, Open Doors audiocassette.

13. Danyun, *Lilies Amongst Thorns* (Tonbridge, Kent, U.K.: Sovereign World, 1993), 30.

14. Report, China Ministry Division of Christian Communications Ltd. (Hong Kong).

15. A missionary, "Answered Prayer," http:www.usmo.com/denny/testimony.htm (May 7, 1999).

16. Oswald Chambers, *Disciples Indeed* (Fort Washington, Pa.: Christian Literature Crusade, 1955), 40.

17. A Chinese missionary trainer, whose name was withheld for security reasons. Interviewed by Alex Buchan. *China Development Brief, No. 49*, Open Doors (August–September 1996).

18. Ron Kernahan, "30 Days Muslim Prayer Focus," Youth With A Mission, http:www.ywam.org/prayer/30days.html (April 28, 1999).

19. Foxe, *Foxe's Book of Martyrs*, 301.

20. Mikhail Khorev, *Letters From a Soviet Prison Camp*, (Eastbourne, U.K.: Monarch Publications, 1986), 9.

21. Brother Andrew, Open Doors letter to supporters, June 1994.

22. Hector Tamez, Audiocassette interview on Open Doors—U.K. Prayertape.

23. Estabrooks, *Secrets to Spiritual Success*, 124.

24. Oswald Chambers, *God's Workmanship* (Fort Washington, Pa.: Christian Literature Crusade, 1953), 136.

25. Estabrooks, *Secrets to Spiritual Success*, 79–80.

26. Alex Buchan, *China Development Brief, No. 57*, Open Doors (August–October 1998).

27. A Henan province itinerant evangelist, whose name was withheld for security reasons. Reported by Alex Buchan. *China Development Brief, No. 54*, Open Doors (August–October 1997).

28. A house church member, whose name was withheld for security reasons. Interviewed by Alex Buchan. *China Development Brief, No. 55*, Open Doors (January–March 1998).

29. Ron Buchan, *China Development Brief, No. 57*, Open Doors (August–October 1998).
30. *Victory in the Battle*, Open Doors U.S.A. seminar publication, 1981.
31. Estabrooks, *Secrets to Spiritual Success*, 157–159.
32. Georgi Vins, *Let the Waters Roar: Evangelists in the Gulag* (Grand Rapids, Mich.: Baker Book House, 1989), 194.
33. Peter de Bruijne, *Siberian Miracle* (London: Marshall Pickering, 1990), 104–106.
34. Paul Estabrooks, personal interview with Pastor Joseph Bondarenko, November 1991.

Thank you for selecting a book from
BETHANY HOUSE PUBLISHERS

Bethany House Publishers is a ministry of Bethany Fellowship International, an interdenominational, nonprofit organization committed to spreading the Good News of Jesus Christ around the world through evangelism, church planting, literature distribution, and care for those in need. Missionary training is offered through Bethany College of Missions.

Bethany Fellowship International is a member of the National Association of Evangelicals and subscribes to its statement of faith. If you would like further information, please contact:

Bethany Fellowship International
6820 Auto Club Road
Minneapolis, MN 55438 USA